OTHER BOOKS BY BARBARA CORCORAN

All the Summer Voices
Don't Slam the Door When You Go
Sam
This Is a Recording
A Dance to Still Music
The Long Journey
Meet Me at Tamerlaine's Tomb
A Row of Tigers
Sasha, My Friend
A Trick of Light
The Winds of Time

AXE-TIME,
SWORD-TIME

Barbara Corcoran

AXE-TIME, SWORD-TIME

ATHENEUM 1976 NEW YORK

Library of Congress Cataloging in
Publication Data

Corcoran, Barbara.   Axe-time, sword-time.
Summary: On the eve of World War II a young girl
handicapped by a reading disability tries to cope
with family problems and the question of her future.
[1. Reading disability—Fiction. 2. World War,
1939-1945—Fiction] I. Title.
PZ7.C814Ax   [Fic]   75-29468
ISBN 0-689-30498-6

Copyright © 1976 by Barbara Corcoran
All rights reserved
Published simultaneously in Canada by
McClelland & Stewart, Ltd.
Manufactured in the United States of America
Printed by Sentry Press, New York
Bound by The Book Press, Brattleboro, Vermont
Designed by Suzanne Haldane
FIRST EDITION

1895310

ACKNOWLEDGMENTS:

I should like to thank *Richard Gercken,* reference librarian
at the University of Montana Library, for helping me
find material I needed. My thanks also to *Mary Conley,*
for helping me remember how it all was, and to
Rosalie Tinkham for providing me with numerous
newspaper accounts of the proximity fuse.

The passage from
"The Short Happy Life of Francis Macomber"
by Ernest Hemingway is reprinted
courtesy of Charles Scribner's Sons.

FOR RUTH GAGLIARDO,
who has done so much to encourage
both the readers and the writers
of children's books.

"Hard it is on earth . . .
  Axe-time, sword-time . . .
  Wind-time, wolf-time, ere the world falls,
  Nor ever shall men each other spare."

—FROM THE VIKING EDDAS

AXE-TIME,
SWORD-TIME

CHAPTER ONE

Elinor sat huddled on the turn of the wide stairs, out of sight from downstairs, the place she and her brother Tom had sat and listened to the grown-ups ever since she could remember. It was time she quit it; she was grown-up herself—eighteen in November—but she still did it now and then, like her other bad habits, chewing on her thumbnail, losing her temper, not picking up her room.

It was the end of the long Labor Day weekend, warm, with a light sea breeze from the east. Elinor had gone to Marblehead with her father in the afternoon to watch the sailboat races. She felt pleasantly sunburned and tired.

3

It had been a good day. But tomorrow school would begin. She hunched her shoulders at the thought, all the old bitterness and frustration welling up and threatening to spoil her, day.

By now she was supposed to be through with high school, ready to start college. But no such luck. She was doomed to a post-graduate year at the same old school, where it seemed to her she had known nothing but defeat and disappointment.

She hadn't expected to make it to Smith, her mother's college, though she had thought there might be some place, somewhere, that would take her. But her high school record wasn't good enough for any place so she would be back for another year trying to improve it, trying to do the impossible. If the family would only face the fact that she was never going to succeed academically, and let her do something else. When she said that, her mother always said, "Such as what, Elinor?" And all Elinor could think of was clerking in the dime store or being a waitress, possibilities that her mother found too distressing even to discuss. "Try to remember," she always said, "you are Dr. Golden's daughter and Judge Cross's granddaughter." Her mother refused to admit that anything was wrong with Elinor that couldn't be cured with a little effort. Her father knew better, but he, too, kept hoping for some miracle. Nobody was even exactly sure what was the matter with her, except that an accident, a crazy, ludicrous accident, had apparently damaged some tiny little place in her brain, so that she had great trouble reading and writing and seeing things the way other people saw them.

Downstairs her mother was entertaining the local Bundles for Britain group at a tea. The women were knitting and eating and chattering like mad. It amazed her that any of them ever heard what anyone else said, since they all seemed to talk at once. She wondered what the English flyers, for whom they were busily knitting scarves and sweaters, would think of them. England had been at war with Germany for two years now. And still we all sit around drinking tea, Elinor thought, and knitting things they probably don't even want; we've made something romantic out of it. And our lives go on as they always have. She worried a lot about the war, and yet she realized that to her, too, it seemed romote. Her brother Tom talked about quitting college to enlist in the RAF, but she didn't think he meant it.

She stiffened as she heard her name in the babble of voices. Someone was asking her mother if she was going to college. That would have to be someone who didn't know them very well, probably that Mrs. Harrison, who was new in town. Everybody else knew that Elinor Golden was too stupid to get into college.

Her mother's usually low, cultured voice was raised a little to be heard above the hubbub. "We're keeping her with us another year," she said, with that little laugh that meant whatever she wanted it to mean. "She needs to brush up on some of her subjects."

Elinor could imagine the faces of the others, smiling, embarrassed, or superior, depending on who it was. Then she heard her mother add: "Tom seems to be the scholar in the family. Elinor is the active one."

Elinor got up and climbed the rest of the stairs to her room. People who eavesdrop, she reminded herself, hear no good about themselves. She turned on the big, dome-shaped radio by her bed and let it warm up. She threw herself down on the bed without bothering to turn back the bedspread, a habit her mother hated.

The radio came on, playing a Paul Whiteman record, which she only half listened to. It was interrupted by a news bulletin on the latest successes of the Nazi armies in their drive into Russia, an invasion already three months under way. Elinor found it bewildering. Such a short time ago the Germans and Russians had been allies. She listened, trying to make sense out of it. So many countries were involved in war and it was all so complicated. She had a National Geographic map of Europe on her wall, and she tried to keep track of what was happening, but usually her father or Tom had to explain it to her. Because it took her so long to read all the names of the countries, she memorized their colors on the map.

She lay back, listening to H.V. Kaltenborn's tense voice describing the situation. No matter how hard she tried to picture it all, it seemed so far away from her life. Restlessly she twisted the old Tom Mix horseshoe nail ring that she still wore on her little finger. Her mother had given her a pretty ruby for her birthday last year, but Elinor left it in its little padded box and went on wearing the horseshoe nail. She knew it was childish and unreasonable, but much of the time she felt childish and unreasonable. Why pretend everything was dandy?

When her mother called her for dinner, she pretended to be asleep. Later she would go down to the kitchen and finish off the tea sandwiches. Dinner had become a tense affair, and she didn't feel like facing it tonight.

Kaltenborn was describing British-German air battles over the channel, and he recalled a speech Churchill had made a year ago when the RAF was fighting for England's life: " 'The gratitude of every home in our Island, in our Empire, and indeed throughout the world, except in the abodes of the guilty, goes out to the British airmen who, undaunted by odds, unwearied in their constant challenge and mortal danger, are turning the tide of the World War by their prowess and their devotion. Never in the field of human conflict was so much owed by so many to so few.' "

And we knit them sweaters, Elinor thought. If only there were something real that she could do, something that mattered. She circled the places on the map that the Germans had advanced to in Russia. It took her several minutes to find Kiev. Such a little name among all those long ones. She sat down on her bed afterward and tried to see the word in her mind. It should be easy enough. K-i-v-e? K-e-. . . She gave up.

CHAPTER TWO

"How did the day go?" her father asked, after the first day of school.

He had just come in, having missed dinner again. He sat at the rolltop desk in the little office that he kept in the house. He was head anesthesiologist at the hospital, and most of his time was spent there. Elinor's mother, who wanted the little room for a sewing room, often pointed out that he didn't need an office at home. But he had always had it, and Elinor was sure he would keep it. Especially now, because more and more he closed himself into that small room when he was at home. Not that he was home very much any more. The younger men on the staff had enlisted, leaving Dr. Golden in constant demand.

And he doesn't like to be home, Elinor thought uneasily, watching his tired, worried face. For a long time now her parents had been having trouble getting along with each other. They didn't talk about it in front of Elinor and Tom, but a person couldn't help knowing, if he had eyes and ears. Raised voices, slammed doors, hostile silences, her mother's tear-stained face. It worried Elinor that her father might leave, and then with Tom and Jed and Julie all away, she wouldn't have a friend left.

"It was all right," she said, answering his question. "The first day is chaos anyway. The math teacher has resigned to join the Canadian Air Force." She grinned, waiting for him to share her relief at the departure of the hated math teacher; but he only nodded absently.

"Who have you got for English?"

"Somebody new. I think her name is Jones."

He did smile this time. "One of those unusual names."

She felt better when he smiled. It scared her when he was remote. He never used to be, unless he was worrying about a patient, but lately he often seemed to be on another thought track that she couldn't reach. "Do you think we'll get into the war?"

"Oh, sure. It's a matter of months or weeks now. We're in it all but official declaration. The Atlantic Charter after all . . . Churchill and Roosevelt weren't sitting out there playing pinochle."

"Somebody on the radio said we've got almost a million men in the armed forces already. I hope they don't draft Tom."

"So do I."

"I don't see how we can stay out very long," he went

9

on. "We aren't about to sit here and let England go down the drain." He pushed his hair back from his forehead. He really did look tired. "You'd better have a talk with this Miss Jones."

"What'll I say?" It made her nervous to think of it.

"Well, tell her you've got a reading problem, always have had. . ."

"Not always," Elinor said, a little defensively. "You said yourself I was a very good reader till I was knocked out."

"That's right. Yes, you were." He frowned, as if he were trying to remember something or figure something out. "Explain to her that you were knocked out by a golf ball. . . ."

"I can't do that," she said sharply.

"Why not, Ellie?"

"People laugh if I say that. You can't go around saying 'I was a real bright kid till I got whacked on the head by a golf ball'. . . I mean, they laugh."

"People are idiots," he said. "You can't pay attention to people like that. There's nothing funny about a concussion. There's nothing in the least funny about being in a coma for twenty-four hours."

"And coming out of it a moron," she said bitterly.

"Don't talk that way. You're no moron, and you know it. You have a very high I.Q. You're a very bright girl. But there was obviously some kind of damage in the temporal lobe that makes reading and conceptual learning hard for you. We simply have to learn how to handle that."

It made Elinor feel terrible when he talked about her as if she were a patient. He seldom did it. "What am I doing wasting another year in high school?" she said.

"Dear, we've been all over that." He tipped his chair back and frowned at the wall. "Your mother wants you to go to college. . . ."

"You know I can't get into college. It's all a big bunch of baloney. Why doesn't Mother face it?" And why don't you help me, she wanted to cry out. You know what the facts are. Why do you let them put me through this? But he'd be upset if she said that. As he said, they'd been through it, over and over. He simply didn't know what to do about her.

"I keep reading the medical journals," he said, nodding at a stack of AMA journals on the table, "praying somebody will come up with some answers. I know they're looking. There's so much that's not understood about the brain. But I *know* something can be done. . . ." He got up abruptly and took her hands in his. "Don't give up, honey, Just don't give up. I'll find the answers if it's the last thing I do." He leaned over and kissed her forehead. "You're a good brave girl and I love you." He turned away quickly, but she saw the tears in his eyes.

She got up, feeling heavy and depressed. Sometimes her inadequacy drove her into a rage, but more often it just seemed like a huge stone tied around her neck, keeping her from the life she wanted to live.

"Well, don't worry about it," she said, trying to sound reassuring. "I've made it this far."

He followed her to the door and gripped her shoulder. "Just don't forget, Ellie, I love you. No matter what happens."

Frightened by his tone, she said, "What's going to happen?"

"No, no, I didn't mean to scare you. It's just that. . .

these are very unsettled times. In the world and in our own house. I want you to remember that I love you and you can always count on me."

She went slowly outside and walked down the sloping lawn to the hedge. From here she could see the ocean. It looked black and quiet tonight. The ocean could be a friend, and it could be frightening and threatening. She thought of the reports of German U-boats in the waters off the coast. Nobody knew if they were true or just rumors. You couldn't tell because the government kept it all hush-hush.

What had her father meant about "no matter what happens"? Was he thinking about leaving? She shivered. She wished Tom were home. She needed to talk to him. Tom always thought things were going to turn out for the best. Sometimes that annoyed her but there were other times when that was what she needed to hear.

 CHAPTER THREE

Miss Jones had asked her to stay a moment after class. She was looking at Elinor's paper. Then she looked up with a friendly smile. Miss Jones was the youngest teacher Elinor had ever had, and she wasn't sure yet what she thought of her. That big friendly act might be phony.

"I have a problem, Miss Golden," she said. She called her students "Miss" and "Mr." as if they were already in college.

Elinor waited. She knew what was coming. She'd been hearing it for six years.

13

"You have interesting ideas, original ideas, but when it comes to getting them on paper, the mechanics . . ." She shook her head. "Sentence structure, development of ideas, spelling . . . Oh, my! the spelling!"

Elinor gave her a wan smile. "I'm sorry. I can't spell."

Miss Jones laughed. "That's the understatement of the year." She turned and wrote "brother" on the blackboard. "What's that?"

Elinor looked at it for a moment, spelling it out to herself. "Brother."

Miss Jones handed her the chalk. "You write it."

Unwillingly Elinor stepped to the board and wrote "b-o-r-t-h-e-r."

"Miss Golden! Look what you've written."

"'Brother,'" Elinor said. She felt humiliated.

"Spell it out for me."

"B-r-o-t-h-e-r."

"Is that what you've written?"

Elinor threw down the chalk. "Yes!" Rising anger made her feel suffocated. In a minute she'd lose her temper and get sent to Mr. Whittier and all that would start again. Her mother would throw a fit and her father would look sad and . . . oh, hell! "I can't spell," she said. "You may as well get used to it." She turned on her heel and started for the door.

"Miss Golden!" Miss Jones's tone was sharp.

Surprised, Elinor stopped and looked at her.

"Come back here and sit down. And don't walk out again when I'm talking to you."

Elinor was astonished. The mild, smiling Miss Jones, just out of teachers' college, talking to her like that? She came back and sat down. "Sorry."

Miss Jones turned her back and erased the two words on the blackboard. Elinor got the impression that Miss Jones was fighting to control her own temper. Although she hadn't meant to, Elinor laughed.

Miss Jones whirled around. "Something amuses you?"

A little scared by the blaze of anger in the teacher's vivid blue eyes, Elinor said, "No, I'm sorry. I mean yes, it just struck me funny that I was mad at you and we're both trying not to lose our tempers. . . ."

Miss Jones gave her a long, hard stare, and then unexpectedly she laughed. "Shall we declare a truce?"

"Yes." Elinor felt a lot better. At least this teacher was treating her like a human being. Maybe she ought to do what her father said, tell Miss Jones about her accident and her problems since then. But she couldn't bring herself to do it.

"I've got a good book on spelling at home," Miss Jones said. "It's designed for people who didn't learn to spell. I'll lend it to you."

"Thank you," Elinor said, "but it won't do any good."

"It will if you'll try." She sounded impatient again. "You mustn't be so defeatist." She picked up Elinor's paper and looked through it. "Your sentences need work. You use simple sentences, like a preschool child's book. Try for complex and compound sentences. Develop your thoughts, and the sentence structure will naturally follow."

Elinor listened, but she knew she couldn't do it. She had trouble reading complex sentences, let alone writing them. Miss Jones was quite pretty, she thought, as the teacher went on talking about the need for developing her ideas. That combination of black hair and blue eyes was nice. She couldn't remember ever having a pretty teacher before, although Mr. Bessinger, the math teacher, had been very good looking. She hated him though because he made fun of her stupidity in math. She could add in her head "like a house-afire," as her father said, but she couldn't do anything written right. Elinor Golden, the human adding machine.

"You aren't listening," Miss Jones said. "You're daydreaming."

Elinor jerked her attention back to her teacher. "Yes, I'm listening."

"You daydream a lot, don't you."

Elinor shrugged. "I guess so."

Miss Jones studied her a moment. "That's all for today." She handed her the corrected theme. "I'll bring that spelling book tomorrow."

"Thank you." Elinor escaped as fast as she could without being rude. It was nice of Miss Jones to be interested in her, but Elinor didn't want people to be interested. They were only disappointed in the end, and that made her feel bad.

Jed was waiting for her out at the bike rack. "Where've you been?" he said. He sat astride his bike, resting his elbows on the handlebars. Jed was the son of Dr. Winslow, the general practitioner, and he had been one of her very best friends since they were babies. He had graduated from high school last June, like all her other friends, and in a couple of weeks he would be leaving for college. It was going to be a terrible year, with everybody gone, especially Julie way off in California. Julie always cheered her up.

"The new English teacher kept me after."

He made a face. "One of those."

"Well, she means well, I guess. She's under the false impression that I'm brighter than I seem." She laughed. "Wait till she finds out."

Jed frowned. "You're bright, and you know it."

"Thanks. Nobody but you and my father seem to be in on the secret." She put her books in the basket of her bike. "Where are we going?"

"I've got a new Count Basie record. You want to hear it?"

"Sure."

They rode their bikes up the elm-lined street to the house where the Winslows lived. Elinor loved the house; it was one of the handsomest in town. Jed's father's office was over the two-car garage.

Jed and his younger brother had adjoining bedrooms in the wing at the back. Jed's room was almost as familiar to Elinor as her own. She flopped down on the big leather chair that Jed's father had turned over to him when it began to crack. It was still wonderfully comfortable.

Jed wound up the portable phonograph and put the record on the turntable. His mother appeared in the doorway with a plate of cookies.

"Hi, Ellie," she said. "How's school?"

"Terrible."

She laughed and put the cookies on the barrel that Jed used for a table. "You kids hungry?"

"You know it," Elinor said. "Thanks, Mrs. Winslow." She liked Jed's parents. And Mrs. Winslow was famous for her cookies and cakes.

When his mother was gone, Jed started the record.

Elinor leaned back, listening intently. Music was one thing she could still enjoy. You didn't have to use whatever it was in your brain that governed your reading and writing ability, to enjoy music. She loved swing, and Count Basie was her favorite next to Benny Goodman.

She took a big bite out of the peanut butter cookie. She felt more at peace in the Winslow house than she did in her own. Than she did anywhere, in fact. She wondered if Mrs. Winslow would mind if she dropped in now and then when Jed was gone.

Tapping her foot to the beat of the music, Elinor contentedly ate cookies and looked around the room. There was the carefully-framed typed excerpt from the letter of an American boy who had died with the Abraham Lincoln Brigade fighting Franco in Spain: Jed had copied it from a newspaper. "June 22, 1938: About myself, I am doing fine, a good shot really, like a Coney Island range expert. This summer may well seal the fate of world peace. Everybody must be brought to the realization that every day Spain continues in its efforts, time is gained for the peace forces all over. In this light Spain is holding the fort for America. If America does not rally it is cutting its own throat." And underneath the paragraph Jed had printed "Wilfrid Mendelson, Brooklyn, killed in action July 28, 1938. NO PASARÁN! " Jed felt very strongly about the war in Spain because his favorite cousin had been killed there, fighting with the Americans in the Lincoln Brigade.

Well, America had not rallied to Spain, Elinor thought, except for that handful of guys in the Brigade. Have we cut our own throat? Elinor thought about it a minute, then she gave her whole attention to Count Basie's brilliant riffs on the piano.

When the record came to a stop, they sat in pleasant silence for a minute.

"Think you could get away to go to Hampton Beach Saturday night?" Jed said. "The old Chick Webb band is going to be playing, with Ella. It's the last bash of the season."

"Oh, Mother's *got* to let me go," Elinor said. "I've got to hear Ella Fitzgerald." But she knew it would mean a big argument. Her mother hated to have her go to dance halls, even with Jed. Only twice had she been able to talk her into it, and that was with help from her father and her brother. "I'll get Dad and Tom to go to bat for me."

"Give her the pitch about how it's our last date before I go away. Do a tearjerker." He put on a recording of Martha Tilton singing "And the Angels Sing," with the Benny Goodman band.

When it was over, Elinor said, "You know what? I'm not going to ask her. I'm just going to go."

Jed looked startled. "Honest?"

"Why not? If I were in college, which I'm supposed to be by this time, I could go out on a date without having to ask my mother. So I'll just go."

"You'll have to account for not being home though. Remember, it's a long drive to Hampton Beach. We'll be late getting back."

"I'll think of something," she said. She took another cookie and smiled. Elinor Golden's declaration of independence.

CHAPTER FOUR

In the beginning it looked as if getting away for the date with Jed wasn't going to be quite as easy as Elinor had thought. First of all, her parents had a battle on Friday night, that for once they didn't even try to conceal from the children. Elinor's father stormed out of the house late Friday night and did not come back. Her mother divided her time between weeping in her bedroom and talking to close friends on the telephone in a hushed voice, as if someone had died.

"She's afraid people will hear about the fight from Dad," Tom said to Elinor, "or at least start imagining things if he's away from home. So she wants to get her innings in first."

But Tom did not stay around long enough to be of any help. His girl's parents had invited him to Newport for a sailing weekend, and he left early Saturday morning. Elinor tried to tell him she was going to cut out for the evening without telling her mother, but he was in a hurry, and all he said was, "Cover your tracks and have a good time." Then he roared off in his yellow convertible.

It's all very well for him, Elinor thought; boys can get away with things. Sometimes she hated being a girl because it seemed to her that she was trapped by convention and custom. If a boy, for instance, had her problems in school, everybody would be perfectly willing to accept it. "He's just not the studious type," they'd say, almost as if it were a compliment.

Then after worrying about it all day, Elinor found her plan unexpectedly easy. Her mother took to her bed with one of her sick headaches. Elinor fixed the toast and tea that her mother ate on such occasions, and took it up to her room. Her mother was lying on one side of the big four-poster bed with a wet washcloth covering her eyes. A bottle of aspirin and a thermos of water were on the bedside table.

"I've brought you some toast and tea," Elinor said softly. She had never been sure whether her mother's headaches, which sometimes seemed so well-timed, were real or faked. Tom said she used them to get attention, but Elinor thought that if that were true, her mother was making a bad mistake. It was no way to appeal to a doctor, who had spent his day looking after sick people.

21

Her mother took the washcloth off her face and looked at Elinor suspiciously. "Are you planning to go out?"

Elinor had told Jed she would have to go in a sweater and skirt, because if she dressed up her mother would notice; but she did have on her new cashmere sweater, which she wouldn't ordinarily wear on a Saturday night unless she were going somewhere.

"Just out with Jed a while," she said. "It's the last time before he leaves for college."

"I was hoping you'd be home," her mother said in a weary voice. "My head is killing me."

"The house is quieter when I'm gone," Elinor said, repeating something her mother often said. "Can I get you anything else before I go?"

"No, nothing. Has your father called?"

"No."

Tears filled her mother's eyes, and Elinor felt a quick wave of sympathy. "He'll be back soon. Don't worry, Mother."

Her mother turned her head away. After a minute of hesitation Elinor left the room. As she was closing the door softly, her mother called to her.

"Don't be late. Where are you going?"

Elinor almost weakened. They could just go to the movies. It seemed cruel to defy her mother now when she was feeling bad. But she was so often feeling bad! If Elinor waited until her mother had nothing to complain about, she'd never break loose. "I'll have to see what Jed says," she answered. It wasn't quite a lie, but it was close, and she didn't feel good about it.

She went downstairs quickly to avoid further questions. She fixed herself a tuna fish sandwich while she waited for Jed. Eating, she wondered where her father was and if he really would come back. If he didn't, she didn't think she could stand it.

When Jed came, Elinor left a note, which she had laboriously printed, on the cork bulletin board for her mother. "Mother: May be a bit late. Don't worry. Didn't want to distrub you. Elinor."

Jed read it over her shoulder and chuckled. "Life, liberty, and the pursuit of happiness."

But Elinor didn't feel especially happy about her act of independence. It seemed sneaky. "I'm not exactly going out with a blare of trumpets," she said.

It was impossible to stay depressed long this evening, however. Jed was in high spirits, and they were going to dance to the late, great Chick Webb's band and listen to Ella in person. Elinor had every record she could find of Ella Fitzgerald's from "A-tisket, A-tasket" on.

Jed put the top down on his old Chrysler convertible. The warm air rushed past their faces. Elinor slid down till she could lean her head back on the leather seat and look up at the dark branches of the elms and maples that bordered the road, making an arch overhead. Through the trees she could see the deep blue-black sky blazing with stars.

They drove along the shore road, with the sound of the ocean more felt than heard. When they crossed the state line into New Hampshire, Jed stopped for a few minutes so they could watch the moon come up out of the sea. They got out of the car and ran across the packed damp sand at Seabrook. Jed caught her hand, and they raced to the foamy edge of the surf. Elinor took off her shoes and socks. The cold wet sand felt good on her bare feet. She dug her toes in and let the thin tide splash over her ankles. The orange moon hanging on the horizon looked enormous.

"After Hampton Beach, let's go to the moon," she said.

"Right. Great idea. I had the sparkplugs cleaned today—the old buggy ought to make it."

She flung out her arms. "Oh, who needs a car. We'll just float up."

He put his arm around her and gave her a hard hug. "You're a nut, and I'm going to miss you."

It was only recently that Jed ever did anything like that. Their relationship had always been more like brother and sister. It disconcerted her a little because it required a change in her own attitude. Up till now her romantic longings had been directed most often at older boys who hardly knew she existed.

But the moment passed quickly without any need of a response on her part. Jed said, "We'd better get going," and started back toward the car. It occurred to Elinor that perhaps he didn't know quite what to do with this new element in their friendship, either.

The huge dance hall at Hampton Beach was already packed with couples, and the band was swinging with a version of "Sunrise Serenade." Jed bought a strip of tickets, and they went out onto the floor. They were both good dancers, and they had danced together so much, Elinor almost knew what Jed was going to do before he did it. When Ella sang "You Must Have Been a Beautiful Baby," they found a place close to the bandstand and danced in place, hanging on every note. Then in a change of mood, Ella sang "I Didn't Know What Time It Was," from the Rodgers and Hart show *Too Many Girls,* which Jed had taken Elinor to see in Boston.

At the end of the number, while the band went out

24

for a break, Jed and Elinor bought Cokes and sat on a wooden bench at the edge of the dance floor.

"Gosh, this is one of the greatest nights of my life," Elinor said. "Isn't it wonderful?"

"You bet. I'd rather be me than Prince Obolensky."

Elinor giggled. "I'd rather be me than Brenda Frazier. Than Barbara Hutton. Than . . . than who? Doris Duke."

"You're throwing away an awful lot of money there, girl."

Elinor made a lavish gesture, spilling her Coke. "It's nothing." She took Jed's proffered handkerchief and mopped up the Coke on her skirt. She felt so happy, even school seemed far away, a faint cloud somewhere in the distance that might disappear if she didn't look at it. And her father. . . . She refused to think about it. He would be home when she got home. He had to be.

Later they danced to a slow waltz. The lights in the hall were turned out except for the huge slowly revolving chandeliers that threw multi-colored lights over the dancers and the hall. It was like dancing through pieces of a rainbow. Elinor leaned her head against Jed's shoulder, and he held her tight. She felt like Adele Astaire, and Jed was Fred Astaire. We're famous dancing stars, she thought, and we're in the movies.

She hated to have the evening end. There might never be another one like it.

"You'll probably fall for some real vampy girl when you get to Dartmouth," she said as they started the drive home.

Jed laughed. "I don't think they've got too many vamps in Hanover. From what I hear, the only time you see a girl is at Winter Carnival."

25

Elinor held her breath, hoping he was going to ask her to Winter Carnival. She'd hoped that ever since he decided to go to Dartmouth. But he hadn't asked her, and he didn't ask her now. Maybe he had somebody else in mind. Or maybe he thought she was too young. After all, she was still in high school. The thought ate away at her happiness. She tried to forget it.

They drove in silence for a while. When they got to Salisbury, Jed said, "Hey, let's ride the roller coaster."

"Is it open?"

"The lights are still on." He swung down the street that led to the amusement park. The ticket booth was lighted, and the man who sold tickets sat there reading a paper. No one else was around. "Can we get a ride?" Jed asked him.

He looked at them over his glasses. "If you want." He took their money, and they got into the front seat of the roller coaster.

Elinor felt queasy as she looked at the long loops and spirals of the track. Roller coasters scared her to death, but she always wanted to go for the ride when there was a chance. She'd never sat in front before, and it was eerie to be the only ones on the little train.

She clutched Jed's arm as the train jerked and started along the track. "Yike! I'm scared!" She closed her eyes as they came to the first steep dip. She'd discovered that if she closed her eyes before the fall began, her stomach didn't do that crazy sinking. It was really strange riding the roller coaster in the dark.

When it was over, she felt a little sick and unsteady, but it had been fun, an unusual experience that she wouldn't forget.

"You look pale," Jed said. "Are you all right?"

"Sure." She held his hand as they walked back to the car. It was nice to be looked after. "Don't go away," she said impulsively. Then she laughed to show she was joking.

"Listen," he said, "I'll write every week. Will you?"

She was silent for a moment. "Jed," she said finally, "you wouldn't like my letters. I can't write a decent letter."

"I didn't think." He squeezed her hand. "Listen, I'm going to write to you anyway, and you write whatever you feel like. Or call me up."

"Will you have a phone?" It was humiliating to think she couldn't even write to him.

"They have phones on the floors of the dorms. Anyway I'll probably make a fraternity. At least I hope I will. We'll work it out. Don't worry." He opened the car door for her.

She was quiet on the drive home. It seemed there were so many things in life other people took for granted, that she couldn't do. A simple thing like writing to your friend. She felt like crying. She thought of the golfer whose ball had hit her in the head, and she wanted to kill him. But they had never even known who it was. She had been playing golf with her father with her new small-sized clubs, and he had been so concerned with getting her to the hospital after she was knocked out, he had never discovered whose ball had hit her. Not that it really mattered. She put her hand to her head in an impatient gesture, angry at that brain that didn't work right.

"When you're a doctor, maybe you can fix my head," she said, trying to make it sound like a joke.

He reached for her hand. "You'll get it fixed long

27

before that. My dad and your dad will come up with something. Or find somebody who has. My dad is always looking for new developments that might help you."

"I know," she said.

"Just don't get discouraged, Ellie. You're a wonderful girl. You're the greatest girl I know."

"But what's going to become of me?" She hadn't meant to say that, but his sympathy was too much for her. She bit her lip to keep from crying.

"Just keep doing the best you can."

She sighed. She couldn't expect Jed to come up with miracles. Nobody could help her because there wasn't any help. She'd probably end up living at home with her mother, helping her keep house and hating it.

When Jed walked her to her door, she braced herself for a scene with her mother. The lights were on all over the house. Her mother was in the living room, sitting on the sofa in her negligee, crying. Elinor's father was coming down the stairs with a suitcase, looking grim.

As soon as Jed had gone, Elinor's mother said, "Your father is leaving us."

CHAPTER FIVE

Elinor leaned against the door. She felt a little the way she had on the roller coaster when it plunged down and down into the dark, only now there was no upward swing to follow and no one to cling to. She looked at her father, and he looked back at her with bleak, unhappy eyes.

"Walk out to the car with me, Ellie," he said.

"Don't try to swing her over to your side," Elinor's mother said, in a sharp, unnatural voice. "It won't work, you know. You're abandoning her, too."

He opened the door and waited for Elinor to go ahead of him.

"I'll be back in a minute, Mother," she felt constrained to say. Her mother's face frightened her. She had often felt that her mother dramatized her emotions, built up scenes that were really nothing, but this was real, and the ravages were there in her mother's face.

"I'll never give you a divorce," her mother called. "Don't think you can wear me down."

He turned in the doorway and looked at his wife. His manner was suddenly gentle. "You'll be taken care of, Claire. You'll have the house and all the money you need. . . . "

She interrupted him fiercely. "House! Money! I ask for bread and you give me a stone."

He sighed and followed Elinor into the yard, closing the door. He put his suitcase in the back seat of the car and then sat down heavily on the running board, as if he had run out of strength.

"No matter what she thinks now," he said, "the house and the money *are* important to her. You know that."

Elinor didn't answer. She felt split. She loved her father with all her heart, but at that moment she felt desperately sorry for her mother. Twenty-six years of marriage. . . . And her mother cared about more than the house and the money. She cared very much about her pride. She was the doctor's wife. It was going to be very hard on her to be the doctor's discarded wife. It seemed to Elinor that her father didn't understand that part of it. And they had loved each other once. She remembered that. It was only in the last few years that that had fallen apart, slowly and irreversibly. She looked up at her father and thought that marriage was about the most dangerous thing a person could walk into.

30

He stood up and opened the car door. "Will you come over to the hospital tomorrow and have lunch with me? Come at one." Without waiting for an answer he got into the car and started the engine. There were tears on his cheeks.

Elinor wanted to say something comforting, but she couldn't think of anything. As he drove away, she watched the cadeusus on the back of his car until she couldn't see it any more. He had dropped his hat on the ground when he sat on the running board. She picked it up and went into the house.

Her mother had lighted a cigarette. She almost never smoked, except now and then at a social gathering where everyone else smoked. She puffed hard on the cigarette, making little white clouds of smoke. She didn't inhale.

"He'll be back," she said. Her voice was high and tight. "He's just trying to scare me, but he'll be back."

Elinor didn't think so, but she only said, "Why don't you get to bed, Mother. It's late."

Her mother glanced at her as if she were hardly aware of who she was. As she went up the stairs, she said, "I'll have to depend on you now."

Elinor shivered. After her mother had gone, she sat for half an hour in the dark, trying to sort out her feelings, trying to understand what was happening to them all. Then she gave up and went to bed, but she lay awake for a long time.

She slept until eleven the next morning and then woke with a start, feeling that something awful had happened but not for the moment able to remember what it was. When she did remember, she tried to go back to sleep but that didn't work. So she got up and dressed for her lunch date with her father. It was odd to have a date with your own father.

Normally on a weekend she would wear her dungarees, and one of her brother's white shirts, tails out. Her mother never ceased to protest, but it was more or less the standard uniform for girls her age. She knew her father liked to have her look nice when she came to the hospital, though, so she dressed carefully in a tweed skirt and sweater, ankle socks and saddle shoes.

Her mother's bedroom door was closed, and there was no sign in the kitchen that she had been downstairs. Elinor wondered whether she should take her some breakfast, and then decided against it. There would be a scene if her mother learned she was going to lunch with her father. She poured herself a glass of tomato juice and lay on her stomach on the living room floor to look at the comic section of the Sunday paper.

When she left at twelve-thirty, her mother still had not come down, but she heard the water running so she knew she was all right—at least still alive. Her mother had been known to threaten suicide in some of the more violent battles with her husband. Elinor had never taken it seriously, but still, it made her a little uneasy until she knew her mother was up.

She slipped out the back door quietly and started off on the two-mile bike ride to the hospital. She wondered where her father would take her to lunch, and then felt guilty for thinking about such a frivolous thing when everybody was suffering so much. She had learned, though, that there was a limit to how much you could keep your mind on suffering. Normal everyday things kept intruding.

She had to walk her bike up the long hill to the hospital. She leaned it against a tree in the back and went in the doctors' entrance. She passed a couple of nurses and an intern who knew her, and was stopped at the end of the corridor by a Sunday nurse who didn't. But she identified herself and went on to her father's office. He was sitting at his desk, looking tired. He jumped up when she came in.

"Hi. I'm glad you came."

She kissed him. "Did you think I wouldn't?"

"I thought you might get talked out of it." He paused. "How is your mother?"

"I don't know. She was still in her room when I left, but she was taking a shower so I guess she's all right."

He looked relieved. "How do you feel about a shore dinner?" He put on his topcoat. "The restaurants in Essex are still open. How about Callahan's?"

"Oh, that would be nice. Callahan's has the best fried clams in the whole world."

He smiled. "You're an authority on clams, are you?"

"Well, you know what I mean. They're so good, nobody's could be better."

He ushered her out of the office, talking about fried clams. "I don't think you find fried clams in many other places, as a matter of fact. The kind of clam that's good for frying is the littleneck, that you get here in Ipswich . . . Good morning, Miss Haines. Have you met my youngster?"

Miss Haines was the nurse Elinor had just spoken to. She smiled at Elinor and said yes, she had, and then she and the doctor discussed where he would be if he were needed.

The drive along the north shore to the Essex turnoff was especially beautiful that autumn afternoon. They didn't talk about the family situation. They talked about casual things, about Jed's plans for pre-med, about Tom's girl. He asked if Elinor had told Miss Jones about the reason for her reading and writing difficulties.

"No, but I almost did. She's sympathetic and nice."

"Would you like me to talk to her?"

"Oh, no, thanks." That seemed too childish. Already she felt ridiculous, going to school with kids she had always thought of as much younger, although most of them really weren't, not more than a year or two anyway. She couldn't have her parents trotting to school to smooth her path. "I'll tell her sometime."

"What about math?"

She hesitated. "I've been cutting it."

He frowned. "If you're going to do that, why don't you drop it."

"Would you approve my schedule change?" She knew her mother wouldn't. Her mother wanted her to keep plugging away at the courses she would need to take college boards. College boards. It was sad, really, that her mother still clung to that.

"Of course," he said. "You'd have to tell your mother, and there'd be a battle, but I'm damned if you're going to have to go on suffering through things that are obviously not suited to your talents."

"My talents." She laughed sadly. What are my talents, Dad?"

"Now don't start that," he said with a touch of impatience. "You sound sorry for yourself, and you're too good a kid for that kind of easy out."

She felt a little hurt. He seldom scolded her. "Well,"

she said, hoping she sounded the way he wanted her to, "I'm hell on wheels in French conversation. Miss Davis says my accent is better than hers." She laughed. "Which isn't saying much." 1895310

"You've got a good ear," he said. "Languages, music, that sort of thing. Why don't you work on that?"

She didn't risk irritating him again by sounding defeatist, but he was forgetting that to get anywhere in languages or music, you had to be able to read as well as listen or perform. "I'm starved," she said. "I hope Callahan's isn't crowded."

He turned off onto the road that led to Essex, a small town on the tidal river, not far from Gloucester. Callahan's parking lot was full, but not, as she pointed out, "jam full." They arrived at the right moment to get a table by the window, overlooking the river.

From their window they could see the half-finished ships standing like skeletons on their frames. Because of the war they were building boats in Essex again.

Elinor ordered the complete shore dinner, with clam chowder, fried clams, fried lobster, filet of sole, fried shrimp, and French fried potatoes. Her father laughed. "What will you do if the government decides to ration food?"

"They won't, will they?"

"I've heard there's talk of it. But probably not until we get directly involved in the war."

"I couldn't stand it," she said. "I'm hungry all the time, as it is."

"I don't think President Roosevelt will let you starve."

They had a good time together, and later they drove to Gloucester, taking the long way home. When Elinor left her father, he said, "Ask Tom to call me when he gets home, will you?" He kissed her. "Take it easy, honey." He hadn't talked about his leaving home at all. Maybe there wasn't anything more to say.

"Where are you staying?" Elinor asked him. It seemed awful not to know that.

"I slept at the office last night, but I'm going to get a small apartment in Boston."

"Boston!" It seemed so far away. And a memory of her mother accusing him of having a woman friend in Boston flashed through her mind.

"This town is too small for all of us to be living here, under the circumstances. Boston is only twenty miles away, after all. You can come stay with me sometimes, and we'll go to the theater."

Until now the day had been nice, but the phrase "come stay with me sometimes" made him sound so remote, like a distant relative. The reality of his being gone hit her in a devastating delayed shock, as if not until this minute had she really understood it. She left quickly, afraid she was going to cry.

Her mother was in the hall, talking on the phone, still in her negligee. She glanced up as Elinor came in. "Ellie just came in," she said on the phone, "so I'll be all right now . . . Oh, thank you, Edith dear, but I'll really be all right. One has to bear up. . . ." She bit her lip and tears welled up in her eyes. "No, no, I'm going to be fine. Bye-bye, dear."

Elinor looked at her uncertainly, feeling guilty because she had left her alone and resenting being made to feel guilty. "Are you all right?" It was a stupid question, as her mother's half-smile told her.

"Of course. You'd better get your homework done."

"All right." Glad to escape, Elinor went upstairs. Was it always going to be like this? It wasn't she who had precipitated this family tragedy, but she felt like the scapegoat. She opened the book of short stories Miss Jones had assigned and stared at the title of the first story. Slowly she puzzled it out. "The Short Happy Life of Francis Macomber." She sighed and tackled the opening paragraph.

 CHAPTER SIX

It was just getting dark when she heard Tom's car drive in the yard. She ran downstairs and out the back door. It would be better if she told him about their father's leaving; it wouldn't be quite such a shock.

"Hi," she said. "Have a good time?"

He climbed out of the open convertible without bothering with the door. "Very good." He was wearing gray flannel slacks, a red pullover, and on the back of his head a yachting cap.

He's so good-looking, Elinor thought, it's no wonder all the girls from here to the moon are in love with him.

Besides, he was nice. "Didn't expect you so early."

He got his small leather suitcase out of the back of the car. "You should see the boat Sheilah's father's got. What a beauty!"

"Were they nice—her parents?"

"Oh, yeah. We got along like a three-alarm fire." He gave her his quizzical grin. "Only one little problem. Sheilah and I broke up."

"You broke up?" She was surprised. She'd thought he was rather serious about Sheilah, though he hadn't been going with her very long.

"Yep. Smasheroo." He found his tennis racquet under some sweaters and sneakers in the trunk of the car.

"How come? I thought you really liked her."

"I thought so, too. But she'd been holding out on me." He looked more serious. "She's an America Firster."

"Oh, gosh." Tom had strong convictions about world affairs, and he thought America should be in the war helping Britain.

"Yeah. She never got around to mentioning it till today. I guess she thought she had me hooked, so it was safe to bring it up. But she was wrong. When some girl—or anybody else—starts telling me that Hitler has really done a lot for his country, and he's not out to destroy democracy and his anti-Semitism is just English propaganda . . . then bye-bye, baby."

"Did she say all that stuff?"

"At length. Her father was embarrassed. Maybe he agrees with her, but he was nice enough not to argue with his guest. He opened his Chivas Regal for me, and we had a pleasant drink and I shook hands with all three of them and here I am . . . home early." He picked up his suitcase. "*Sic amor transit*. I see Dad is out again." He started to close the garage doors.

"Tom, wait a minute." As he turned toward her, she said, "Dad's left. For good."

Tom put down his suitcase and said, "Oh, lord. Lordy, lordy. It's happened at last. Are you sure it's for good?"

"He says so, and it looks like it. He's going to take a place in Boston to live. He wants you to call him at the hospital."

He glanced toward the house. "How's Mother taking it?"

"Pretty grim."

"Yeah. Well, as Eugene O'Neill would say, 'All God's chillun got wings.' I'd better go see her." He ran up the path silently.

Elinor finished closing the garage doors and picked up his suitcase. In spite of his tone she knew he was upset. He was a lot closer to their mother than Elinor had ever been. She was very proud of her son's good looks and charm, his brains. She was delighted that he was going to enter Harvard Law School when he finished his undergraduate work, and she could hardly wait for him to be a judge. Tom teased her about it but he enjoyed her pride in him. Elinor had never experienced that kind of parental delight, but she thought it was because she hadn't any qualities that deserved it. She was nothing but a disappointment to her mother and a worry to her father. Maybe someday she'd find something she could do well, and they would all suddenly discover her and brag about her. "This is my daugher," her mother would say, "the well-known . . ." But at that point her mind always balked. The well-known what?

She put Tom's suitcase in his room and went to her own. Tom was in their mother's room, and the door was closed. She could hear the low murmur of their voices. After a few minutes she went into the bathroom and took a shower so she wouldn't have to hear them. She stayed in the shower a long time. Then she went downstairs and made herself a jam sandwich.

Tom came in while she was in the kitchen and made some coffee. "Happy times are gone again."

"Is she crying?"

"Not now. I got her a sleeping pill."

"Dad says she takes too many."

"Well, she needs one tonight. It's rough for the old girl."

"I know."

He rattled the percolator impatiently, waiting for it to begin percolating. "It's not going to be any picnic for you after I go back to Cambridge."

"That's all right."

"I was planning to go up tomorrow to get my room in shape, but I guess I'd better put it off a few days."

"It'll be just as hard for her whenever you go."

"Yeah, but I think I'll wait till Wednesday or so." He picked up the coffee pot and peered at it. "What's wrong with this thing?"

"It has to boil," she said. "You can't perk cold water."

"Bad system." He glanced at the book she had brought down with her. "What are you reading?"

She showed him the Hemingway story.

"Oh, that's a good one."

She sighed. "I guess so. It's long. But I've got to get through it. I got bawled out in class the other day for not having read the assignment, and I'd spent two hours on it."

He frowned. "Have you talked to your teacher?"

"Not really."

"I'll come talk to her."

"Oh, thanks, Tommy, but I'll manage."

He picked up the book. "As soon as this stupid coffee perks, I'll read you the story."

She brightened. "Oh, would you? That would be great." When she was younger, after her accident, he often read things to her, and it was he who had helped her train her memory. He read her poems and short pieces of prose over and over until she finally got so she could memorize easily. It was because of her memory that she had managed at all in school. She remembered almost everything her teachers said.

Curled up on the sofa with a fire lighted in the fireplace and Tom reading her the Hemingway story, she almost forgot she had any worries. If only he never had to go away. But everybody she loved went away.

Tom went on reading in his pleasant, deep voice, about the man Macomber who had learned not to be afraid. " 'I'm not really afraid of them now. After all, what can they do to you?' 'That's it,' Wilson said. 'Worst one can do is kill you. How does it go? Shakespeare. Damned good. See if I can remember. Oh, damned good. Used to quote it to myself at one time. Let's see. "By my troth, I care not; a man can die but once; we owe God a death, and let it go which way it will, he that dies this year is quit for the next." Damned fine, eh?' "

It was a sad, sad story, with poor Macomber dead in the end. But he had learned to be brave. That seemed to be what Hemingway was saying: Learn to be brave.

"What does it mean exactly, to be brave?" she said to Tom.

He thought for a minute. "To face up to things? I guess there are different ways of being brave, but that would be one, wouldn't it?"

"I guess that's what's so brave about the English, facing up to the German air attacks without panicking." She thought a lot about the English and tried to imagine what she would do if bombers rained destruction on Massachusetts every night. She could almost hear the deep roar of approaching planes sometimes.

"Would you like to use my shortwave radio while I'm away?" Tom asked.

She was surprised. "I'd love it. But aren't you going to take it to school?"

"No, I spend too much time listening to it if it's there. I've really got to hit the books this year. You can keep it for me."

"Thanks, Tommy. I'll take good care of it."

"I know that." He got up. "And listen, Ellie, don't let all this . . ." he gestured upstairs, "get you down. It's their lives, not ours. They've got to deal with their own troubles."

She nodded. "I know. Only it's kind of our troubles, too."

"Not really. I'm grown-up, you're almost grown-up. We're not dependent on them the way we used to be. Work on your own life."

"If I can figure out what my life is."

He paused in the doorway. "You will. Stop trying to be what Mother wants you to be, to start with. Reading and writing fluently are not the be-all and the end-all of life, for heaven's sake. It's a big world with all kinds of things going on in it. And Ellie, any time you want to, call me up and talk."

She tried to smile. He was a good brother. "Thanks, Tom."

CHAPTER SEVEN

Elinor got her schedule changed the next day so that she was taking just English, French, and chemistry. The student adviser had wanted to talk to Elinor's mother about the fact that she was dropping math, but Elinor had persuaded her not to.

"My mother isn't feeling well," she said. "My father said he'd sign the paper."

Miss Purcell had looked sympathetic. It astonished Elinor that everyone in town seemed to know almost instantly that Dr. Golden had left his wife. It was upsetting. People looked at her oddly, as if to see how she was taking it. And occasionally women she happened to meet downtown would pat her arm and nod. "How is your mother?" they would say mournfully. She knew they meant well but she wished they would leave her alone.

"Your father understands, does he," Miss Purcell was saying, "my point about credits?"

"Yes. It was his idea. I'm a flop in math." There was no point in trying to bamboozle Miss Purcell; she'd been student adviser all through Elinor's high school years. She knew all about her weaknesses.

"All right, I'll approve it, and you have your father sign it then." She gave Elinor one of her rare smiles.

The smile encouraged Elinor to an unusual burst of confidence. "My mother wants me to go to college, but my dad and I are trying to think of something more practical. I'd never make it in college, Miss Purcell."

Miss Purcell didn't commit herself. "It's hard to say. I am afraid you might find it rough going." She handed Elinor the paper. "Come and see me whenever I can help."

After school she took the paper up to the hospital and waited until her father had a spare minute and could sign it. He didn't have time to talk long, but he explained that he was taking Tom to dinner that night. He seemed afraid she would be hurt at being left out. She was not. It seemed quite natural that they might have things they wanted to discuss privately. It was odd, the new etiquette of a father who lived away. None of them had adjusted to it yet.

She didn't mention the change of schedule to her mother until Tuesday. They were at the dinner table, and

Tom, looking frustrated, was trying to carve the roast beef. His mother had insisted that he sit in his father's place. Elinor could tell it upset him.

"Damn!" he said, as the roast slid half off the platter.

"You're doing beautifully," his mother said. "Just get the fork right down into the meat so it won't skid."

Tom grasped the bone-handled carving fork grimly and stabbed the meat. A tiny shower of red splattered the tablecloth. Elinor giggled.

"It's not as blasted easy as it looks," Tom said, but he grinned at her and then started sawing away with the long knife.

"You go at things so hard," his mother said. "Do it gently."

"I was never cut out to be a surgeon," he said.

His mother shuddered. "Don't be crude, dear." She had pulled herself together quite well in the last day or so. Friends had been dropping in, and even acquaintances. Elinor thought some of them came out of curiosity, looking for morsels of gossip, and she resented them bitterly, but her mother seemed pleased that they came. So lots of cups of tea were poured and sandwiches eaten and a little more knitting done for the boys in the Royal Air Force.

"If you plan to come home this weekend, I'll see about a leg of lamb," their mother said to Tom.

He glanced at her quickly and then gave all his attention to placing a piece of meat on a plate. "You like it rare, don't you, Ellie?"

His mother laughed. "You don't know, after all these years?"

"I've never been in charge," he said. He handed the

47

plate to Elinor. "I can't come home this weekend, Mother. I've got to get settled in."

She looked grieved. "Surely by Saturday . . ."

"Look, I delayed going up till tomorrow. There's going to be a lot to do. Classes start Monday." When she didn't answer, he said, "I'll try to make it the following weekend."

A little drily she said, "Don't put yourself out."

"Oh, come on," he said. "You know I didn't mean that."

Elinor listened uneasily. She had the feeling that her mother, who was always possessive with Tom, was trying to put him in the role of head of the house now. It wasn't fair. He shouldn't have to worry about coming home all the time.

"We need to get the storm windows on," her mother said.

"Mr. Haskell can do that," Elinor said.

Her mother frowned. "Mr. Haskell costs money. I have to be careful of money now."

Elinor wanted to say "That isn't true!" but she held her tongue.

"I'll put them on tonight," Tom said.

"That's absurd. It's almost dark already."

Exasperated, he said, "Damn it, Mother, I'll pay Mr. Haskell myself, if that's the problem. But I can't come home this weekend."

"I can put the windows on," Elinor said. "I've held the ladder for Dad or Mr. Haskell hundreds of times. I know what they do."

"Don't you touch them," Tom said. "They're heavy. You'd break your blooming neck."

"Well, let's don't quarrel about the storm windows on your last night home," his mother said.

Elinor decided it was time to change the subject, to take the heat off Tom. "I've dropped math," she said.

Her mother put down her fork and looked at her. "You're what?" When Elinor repeated it, she said, "Without telling me? On whose authority?"

"I talked to Miss Purcell about it. She saw my point. It's silly to go through math and flunk it again."

"I think that's a swell idea," Tom said.

"You need math for your college boards," her mother said. "Why wasn't the paper sent to me to sign?"

Elinor hesitated. "Dad signed it."

"I see. Have I lost all authority over my children?"

"Mother, if you'd only listen. . . ."

Her mother burst into tears and left the table, clutching her linen napkin. She went into the library and closed the door.

Elinor looked at Tom. "Well, I blew that one, didn't I?"

"Listen, I'll talk to her later. Everything upsets her."

"I've ruined your last night home."

"It wasn't too jazzy to start with. Forget it and enjoy your roast beef—ragged edges and all."

Elinor took a bite of meat without tasting it. "I get the feeling we're pieces in a game of checkers, you and me. They're moving us around."

"Of course they are. I don't suppose they know it, but that's what they're doing. In this town if people get divorced, and you know they practically never do, then it's assumed that one or the other is in the wrong. 'Whose fault is it?' That's what everybody asks. So both of them are jockeying for position, to prove it isn't *their* fault. Whichever one gets the kids to support him—or her—gets points."

"Tom, don't you dare come home this weekend for those stupid storm windows. I'll ask Dad for the money to pay Mr. Haskell."

"Promise you won't try to hassle them yourself. They're really heavy, Ellie, and kind of tricky. You promise?"

"I promise."

He looked at the roast, and his gray eyes narrowed with laughter. "Isn't that a hell of a mess? Sheilah doesn't know what she's escaped. I'll never make a proper head of the house."

"There's more to it than cutting up a roast." Elinor returned his grin. It always made her feel good when he laughed.

He raised his glass of milk. "Here's to love and success."

She giggled and touched his glass with her own. "Here's to my crazy brother."

CHAPTER EIGHT

The autumn weeks drifted by uneventfully. School was frustrating, her mother was moody, but the weather held in Indian summer glory until November.

Elinor walked downtown after school feeling good, on one of the first cold, windy days. She eyed the sky for signs of snow. The skiing season ought to start soon. Already advertisements were appearing in the papers for the Snow Train, that would take weekend skiers to New Hampshire and Vermont. Jed had called a few nights ago and mentioned meeting her at North Conway for a skiing weekend in December. He liked the Eastern Slopes

Inn. Elinor was rather cautious about which ski resorts she went to, because many of them were anti-Semitic. Her father's family background was German, but Golden was often assumed to be Jewish, and because of this Tom had been refused entry to a resort in the Adirondacks the winter before. Their mother had been angry with him for not explaining to the proprietor that he was not Jewish; but Tom and Elinor and their father had argued, with considerable heat, that that was not the point. It was the anti-Semitism they objected to. Tom said it was wicked, just like Hitler. But there was nothing like that at Eastern Slopes.

Elinor stopped at the drugstore for a hot chocolate. She had stayed late at school to work with Miss Davis, the French teacher. Most of the high school crowd who headed for the drugstore after school had gone. Elinor sat down at one of the little wrought iron tables. She liked the drugstore. It was warm, and it had a wonderful smell of chocolate and vanilla. Mr. Conolly, in his white pharmacist's coat, came out and made her hot chocolate for her.

"How you been, Ellie?" he said in his friendly way, as if he had not seen her in a long time, although she stopped at the store almost every day.

"Fine, Mr. Conolly. How are you?" She looked at the case full of penny candy and remembered how she and Jed used to stop there after school and spend forever trying to make up their minds how to spend two or three pennies. She had usually settled for penny Tootsie Rolls, and Jed would get licorice whips. Those were the days before her accident, the part of her life that she thought of as carefree and happy.

"Ed Murrow said last night the Germans are bogging

down in Russia," he said, bringing her the foamy hot chocolate. "Were you listening on your shortwave?"

"No, I was studying late. Oh, I hope they are."

He leaned on one of the little chairs, shaking his head. "I was at the Civil Defense meeting last night. We'll be in this war before long. Stands to reason."

Someone came in with a prescription, and Mr. Conolly disappeared into the back of the store to fill it. Two senior girls who were in Elinor's chemistry class came in and stood by the magazine rack reading Flash Gordon comic books. Elinor touched her horseshoe nail ring. She really ought to stop wearing it. She knew other kids laughed about it. But they laughed about her anyway. In chemistry class the other day Miss Hart had said in a voice for all to hear that if Elinor wasn't more careful about reading formulas, she would blow them all right through the roof. That had entertained everyone in the room except Elinor. Last year it wouldn't have mattered so much; she had had friends in her class, who would not have laughed. But the classmates she had now she thought of as enemies.

The two girls went out after a few minutes, and Miss Jones came in. When she saw Elinor, she came right over and sat down.

"I wanted to talk to you after class, but you got away before I had a chance."

What now, Elinor thought.

"I met your father last night at the Civil Defense meeting."

"Oh, did you?" Elinor felt vaguely uneasy. What had they said about her?

"He told me some things I hadn't known before. I'm afraid I was not very understanding."

53

Elinor felt embarrassed. "That's all right. You can't understand things you don't know about."

"But I've had enough training to be able to analyze problems better than that . . ." She broke off. "But that's not what I want to talk to you about. I'm in charge of setting up a plane spotters' schedule. My own tour of duty is on Saturday mornings, six A.M. till ten. I'm finding it hard to recruit for that time. We work in teams of two, you know. I wondered if you would be the other half of my team."

"Plane spotting?" Elinor had read about it in the paper. The towns and cities along the coast were setting up a watch for possible enemy planes. The east coast was nervous about surprise attacks. "What do you do exactly?"

"We're going to use the top of the grade school building because it's flat. An operations hut is being set up there now. Spotters volunteer for weekly shifts. As I said, in twos. They watch the skies for planes and report all that they see."

"Report to who?"

"We'll have a direct line in the operations hut connecting us with Army command headquarters where all planes will be plotted on a big map. Any plane that is unidentified, that hasn't filed a flight plan and so on, will be investigated at once." She paused and smiled. "It's kind of exciting."

"It's not just reading with me," Elinor said. "When I see things, I see them differently."

"That doesn't matter as long as *you* know what you see. A P-38 might not look the same to you as it does to me, but all that counts is that you know it's a P-38."

Elinor began to feel excited. It sounded wonderful,

like really being in the Air Corps. But what if she made mistakes?

"Your father says you have an extraordinary memory."

"I can remember pretty well."

"Will you give it a try?"

"What if I made some awful mistake?"

"I'll be there, too, you see. We can double-check on each other."

"All right. I'd like to do it. I really would." There goes the skiing weekend, she thought, but this was important.

"Fine. I'll meet you outside the main door of the school at five of six Saturday morning. Wear warm clothes." She smiled and left.

Some people had come into the drugstore. The owner of the hardware store was buying coffee for the owner of the feed and grain store. They stood at the soda fountain arguing about the war.

"FDR will turn the country over to the British, lock, stock, and barrel," the hardware man was saying. "Mark my words. We'll be right back where we were before 1776."

"Bushwa, George," said the feed and grain man. "We can't let those barbarians take over the world. My boy got his draft notice yesterday, and I want to tell you, I'm proud."

They were still arguing when Elinor left.

That night she turned on the shortwave radio and heard Ed Murrow's impressive voice: "This . . . is London." And as she listened to the news, she thought, I'll be fighting the war, too, in a very small way. She would check out her ski clothes in the morning and see what she should wear.

55

CHAPTER NINE

Although she was ashamed of anything she wrote, she did write a letter to Jed the next night. She had tried to call him at school, but he wasn't in, and she couldn't wait any longer to tell him about plane spotting.

It had been, as she told him, her second declaration of independence. The one when she went to Hampton Beach hadn't really counted because that was the night her father left home, and her mother had never even noticed that she was gone. But this time her mother laid down the dictum: no plane spotting. Her reasons were vague. It would be too cold, and Elinor would catch the flu; it was too early, and it would deprive her of her sleep; Elinor wouldn't like it and would quit.

She listened patiently to her mother's arguments and then she said, "I'm sorry, Mother, but I am going to do this."

Her mother had looked startled. She was not used to defiance. "You don't care about my feelings?"

"I don't think they're good reasons. I'm old enough to decide things like this myself. I want to do it. It's the only thing I can think of to do that will help."

"Hasn't it occurred to you that you might not be up to the responsible task of identifying planes?"

"If I can't do it, of course I'll quit. But I want to find out."

Her mother changed her tactics. She looked hurt and grieved. "It doesn't matter that I'll be worried sick, alone here in this house."

"Mother, be reasonable. What is there to worry about?"

Sharply she said, "For one thing, I know nothing about this Miss Jones."

Elinor began to lose patience. "I suppose if she's fit to teach in the school, she's safe enough to go plane spotting with."

"Not necessarily. Not necessarily at all. There was that gym teacher. . . ."

Elinor sighed. Whenever her mother wanted to cast aspersions on a teacher, usually a teacher that Elinor liked, she brought up the gym teacher who had been fired a few years ago because one of her students had accused her of what the newspaper called "improper advances." Elinor and her friends, who had known the girl, had never believed the story, but the teacher had been dismissed.

"I don't suppose," she said, "that the top of the grade school building in twenty-degree weather is a likely place for seduction, if that's what you have in mind."

Her mother had been angry then. "You were not brought up to talk in that crude way," she said. "It's exactly that kind of thing that makes me worry."

"Well, don't worry." Elinor had started out of the room. She didn't like the conversation. It upset her when her mother resorted to tactics like these.

"You're determined to do this?" her mother had called after her.

"Yes, I am." And Elinor had grabbed her coat from the closet and gone out of the house so she wouldn't have to talk about it any more. She'd walked to the public library and sat at one of the big tables where it was quiet and she could start the letter to Jed. Only a page and a half were finished, not counting the ones she'd torn up, when the lights dimmed to indicate closing time. She folded the letter and put it in her pocket and walked slowly home.

The thermometer outside the railroad station registered twenty-three above. Winter was getting off to an early start. In the morning she would go to the school roof for her first plane spotting experience.

She looked up at the starlit sky and wondered if there were any planes up there now. She didn't know what you had to do when you saw them, except call the command post. Did you have to identify them? Well, tomorow she'd find out. She hoped desperately that she'd be able to do it right.

When she got home, her mother was talking to her friend Louise on the telephone, so Elinor went directly to bed, setting her alarm clock for five-thirty. Then she got up and changed it to five, to allow plenty of time. All her clothes were laid out and ready—her skiing long johns, her ski pants, two sweaters to go under her ski jacket, mittens, heavy socks, hiking boots. She had also put out her binoculars and a flashlight.

The alarm seemed to go off almost as soon as she sank into the comfort of her mattress. She forced herself to get up at once, before she should fall asleep again. No wonder Miss Jones found this a hard time to fill.

She dressed and went downstairs quietly. In the kitchen she found a note from her mother. It said: "If you must do this foolish thing, at least eat some breakfast. Cocoa made and ready to warm up." Two eggs and a half loaf of bread were on the table. She was touched and also a little gleeful. She had won that round. Maybe standing up for your rights wasn't so hard after all. You just had to convince your parents that you weren't a child any more.

Hurriedly she fried the eggs, made toast, and heated the cocoa. She was grateful to her mother. She would probably have grabbed a piece of bread and jam and eaten it on the run, if she had been left to her own devices.

She let herself out the back door and walked fast through the dark streets to the school. It was very cold. She hadn't looked at the thermometer, but it felt like about twenty above.

She got to the school a few minutes early, but then Miss Jones came, almost unrecognizable in a stocking cap, heavy corduroy ski pants, and an old raccoon coat that had begun to shed. She unlocked the big school

59

door, and following the light of her flashlight, they climbed up to the third floor and up a ladder to a trap-door in the roof.

Elinor hadn't stopped to think that another shift would be there ahead of them, so she was surprised to be met by two men heavily bundled up in coats and sweaters; one of them even had an old car robe wrapped around him Indian style. After a moment she recognized them—old Mr. Crow, who used to run the shoe repair shop before he got too ancient, and Harry Bissell, who manned the railroad crossing gates during the day. They both seemed almost too cold to speak.

"Quiet night?" Miss Jones asked them cheerfully.

"Cold night," Harry said. "Yeah, quiet. Not many planes." He took them into the tiny shed, where a small wood-burning stove threw out a little heat if you stood right over it. On an improvised plank shelf stood the telephone. On the wall was a chart with the silhouettes and names of planes. Elinor hadn't realized there would be so many. How in the world was she ever going to memorize all those? She felt panicky.

Harry was explaining to Miss Jones, who already knew, how you just picked up the phone and as soon as you heard an acknowledgement from the command post, you started giving your report.

"Got to do it just like it says," Harry said, enjoying his superior knowledge. "You know the military. See, it tells you here, type of plane, number of engines, location . . . here's how you give 'em location . . ."

"Come on, Harry," Mr. Crow said. He was very tall and thin. His teeth were chattering with the cold.

When they were gone, Miss Jones explained the calling-in procedure to Elinor. "Here's our post number. You give that, and then you fill in the information from this form. As the man said, 'type, number of engines, location,' and so on."

"I'll have to memorize that," Elinor said. "I couldn't read it fast enough. Will you go over it two or three times aloud?"

She frowned in concentration while Miss Jones read off the order of information. "Thanks, I think I've got it. Now give me the number of our post." She held her head between her hands, shutting out everything except what Miss Jones was saying. "I've got it."

"I'll take the north side of the roof, you take this side, and then we can swap later if you want to," Miss Jones said. She went off to the other side.

Elinor scanned the sky. It was just beginning to show a faint tinge of silver at the horizon, but it would be some time yet before it was really light or before the cold began to ease up. She walked up and down on the frosted roof, swinging her arms to get the circulation going. And all the time she kept her eyes on the sky. It should be easy in the dark to spot plane lights. If you were an enemy, though, you'd come in without lights. She lifted one side of her stocking cap a little so she could hear, but her ear soon got so cold she had to switch to the other side.

As she walked up and down, she could see Miss Jones doing the same thing on the other side. With this kind of pattern, they weren't going to get much conversation in. She thought of her mother's fears, or fake fears, and made a face.

Elinor stopped short. Far away, just faintly to be seen,

lights had appeared in the sky. They seemed to twinkle and disappear and reappear, and for a moment she thought they might be stars. But they steadied as she watched, and she saw that they were colored. She raced for the shack and then stopped again. How could she report the plane when all she could see was the lights? She ran around the shack and called to Miss Jones, then pointed to the sky.

For a minute Miss Jones didn't see it. Then she did. "Call up and give our number, and say lights of a plane just barely visible, in a . . ." she hesitated.

"Northeast," Elinor said. "That's northeast."

"Yes, good. Tell them that's all you can see."

Elinor ran to the shack. She felt terribly excited. What if it were an enemy plane and she was the first one to see it? She picked up the phone. She heard the answering voice, and then for a second she panicked because she couldn't remember the call number. She bit her lip and concentrated as the voice on the other end spoke again, impatiently.

She read off the call number. "Plane sighted in the distance, northeast. Lights just visible."

That wasn't the approved form, but what else could you do at night? The voice repeated the information and hung up. She was perspiring from nervousness and from the unexpected heat of the stove. She mopped her face with her mitten and went back outside.

Miss Jones called to her. "All right?"

"All right."

Miss Jones came over to her. "I never would have seen that. You have good eyes."

Elinor was pleased. "We report it again, don't we, if it comes this way?"

"Yes." She stared at the sky. "It seems to be going north, though."

"Yes, it's changed course." Elinor wondered if that was suspicious.

"Keep an eye out for it. But then, I know you will."

Elinor watched the faraway winking light dim and finally disappear. The next spotting station up the coast would be reporting it now, probably. It made her feel like a member of a battalion that was defending the country. It was a good feeling.

She heard and then she saw a small plane not far away, but it was on Miss Jones's side so she just checked to make sure Miss Jones had seen it. It was probably from the local airport, a little Piper Cub maybe. She could see Miss Jones's head silhouetted in the light inside the shack. Scanning the sky with a regular motion of her head, like a searchlight, she remembered a line from one of the poems Tom used to read to her when he was teaching her to memorize. "Then felt I like some watcher of the skies."

The dawn came up cold and gray, but it brought with it an Army plane that she rushed to report. She consulted the big wall chart although she was sure it was a P-38 because of the twin tails. She touched the outline of the picture with her finger, just as Miss Jones came into the shack behind her.

"Oh, sorry, you've got it," Miss Jones said.

"P-38?"

"Right." She went away while Elinor called it in.

When Elinor hung up, she noticed on the desk a hand-sized chart of plane types, arranged in a circle, like a fan. She would ask Miss Jones if she could take one home and memorize the plane types. It worried her to have to check them out on the chart, because even though it only involved a few letters, she might reverse them without knowing it. Maybe it wouldn't matter, but then again, maybe it would. For instance there might really be a plane called the P-83.

The hours went by surprisingly fast. Her face was cold, and she had to keep stamping her feet, but it was not acutely uncomfortable. Of course there would be worse days, winter storms and zero weather once in a while, but the hardship made it all seem more important. Nobody could call her a "sunshine soldier."

After their relief came, Miss Jones walked part way home with Elinor. She had promised to ask Civil Defense for one of those hand charts.

"I noticed you touched it with your finger. Does that help?"

"Yes. It makes me sure of the shape."

Miss Jones looked thoughtful. "Have you ever tried that with words?"

"No. I never thought of it."

"Let's try it sometime and see what happens."

"All right." Elinor had tried so many things, she had no faith in new ones, but she didn't want to dampen Miss Jones's hopes.

When she said good-bye to Miss Jones, the teacher said, "You're going to be a very good spotter, Elinor. You've got the eyesight of an eagle, and you're very diligent."

Elinor thanked her. "I like doing it."

When she came into her house, she found her mother and Tom, who was home for the weekend, dismantling the office. Her father's desk and stacks of books stood in

64

the hall, and Tom was struggling with a big box of files.

"Hi," he said. "How was the plane spotting?"

"Wonderful!" She spread her arms. "I'm an eagle!"

Her mother said, "You look half-frozen."

"No, I'm not. Can I have Dad's desk in my room?"

"I suppose so. I was going to put it in the cellar."

"I need a desk. Wait till I get my first three layers of clothes off, Tommy, and I'll help. We can empty the drawers and take them up separately. . . ."

He smiled at her. "You had a good time, didn't you? You're all aglow."

"She's aglow from being half-frozen," her mother said. And just then Elinor sneezed. "You see? Take a hot tub at once, Elinor."

"As soon as I help get the desk upstairs," Elinor said.

 CHAPTER TEN

By midafternoon Elinor was in bed with a fever. Her mother, torn between sympathy and self-righteousness, brought her toast and a pitcher of grapefruit juice and aspirin. She put her hand on Elinor's head.

"I wonder if I should call Dr. Winslow."

"No, no, it's just a cold." Elinor was furious with her body for betraying her. "It couldn't be from the plane spotting, Mother; it happened too quickly. I probably caught it at school. Everybody's got it."

Her mother shook her head but refrained from arguing. "Tom wanted to take us to dinner tonight, but I'll tell him to postpone it."

"Don't be *silly*," Elinor said. "You and Tom go." It took some, but not too much, persuading before her mother agreed.

Later Tom came in. He looked serious. "I'm sorry you can't go. Listen, we'll bring you a doggy-bag." He tried a grin, but it wasn't his usual spontaneous one. He sat on the edge of her bed. "Is there anything you want?"

"No. I'll sleep, and by tomorrow it will be gone. It wasn't the plane spotting, Tom. She won't forbid me to do it, will she?"

"Not if I can talk her out of it." He hesitated as if he had something on his mind. "Elinor, I was going to spring an announcement at dinner. I'll give you the word now, but don't say anything."

Feeling vaguely alarmed by his seriousness, she said, "What is it? Of course I won't tell."

He got up and walked to the window and looked out. "I've joined the Army Ski Patrol."

"You've what?"

"Yeah. I've joined the Ski Patrol."

"I didn't know there was one."

"Yes. I had a talk with Doug Burckett of the Appalachian Mountain Club—he's one of the committee. The National Ski Association got it all started. You know, after the Finns almost beat the Russians fighting in snow on skis, a lot of people began to think." He was getting enthusiastic as he talked. "It's a whole new thing, Ellie. It's really going to be exciting. I'll have to go through Officers' Training, but then I'll really be in on something, from the ground up." He grinned. "Literally."

"What about college?"

"College can wait. There are more important things on the docket."

"Oh, Mother will go into a decline."

He frowned. "I know. I'll have trouble there. But she'll have to accept it. Mothers all over the world are sending their sons off to war. And when we get into the war, I'd be drafted anyway."

Elinor pulled the blanket up around her shoulders as a chill hit her. "Don't get killed or anything, will you?"

"Hey, you know me better than that. Tom Golden, the boy who always lands on his feet." He patted the bedclothes. "Snuggle up and get well now, and maybe I can take you out tomorrow before I go back."

"When will all this start?"

"I report for duty the day after Thanksgiving. General Marshall is really sold on the idea of a winterized army; he wants to get it going."

Their mother called from downstairs.

"Gotta go," Tom said. "I just wanted you to know."

"Thanks," Elinor said. And when he got to the doorway, she added, "I'm awful proud of you."

He gave her a jaunty wave and a grin and ran down the stairs.

After they were gone, Elinor took some more aspirin, drank a glass of grapefruit juice, and slid down until the blankets came up to her chin, but in a minute she was hot again and had to push the blankets back. She had two strong reactions to Tom's news: a feeling of great pride and a feeling of great fear. She had always known that if war went on long enough, Tom would get into it; but she hadn't expected it yet.

The telephone rang. She got up and went out to get

the phone in her mother's room. It was her father, calling to see how the plane spotting had gone. He was distressed to hear that she had a cold.

"No, it doesn't sound like anything to do with spotting," he said. "You probably picked up a flu germ at school. Ellie, keep warm and stay in bed till your fever's gone. Is your mother there?"

"No, Tom took her out to dinner."

"Well, are you all right, honey?"

"Yes, sure, Dad." She felt terribly lonesome all at once. She wanted to say something about Tom, but she had promised not to tell.

"I'm in Boston. I'll be at the apartment all evening. If you feel any worse, call me, Ellie. Promise? Drink a lot of liquids."

She promised and went back to bed.

About an hour later she heard the front door open. She wondered if her mother and Tom were back already. Maybe her mother had fallen apart when she heard Tom's news.

But in a moment she heard Dr. Winslow's deep voice from the downstairs hall. "Ellie, it's Dr. Winslow. May I come up?"

"Sure. Come up." She was glad he had come. He always made her feel better just by being there.

He came into the room, a tall, broad-shouldered man with thick gray hair and a slow, easy manner. "Your dad called. Said you weren't feeling too chipper."

"Oh, it's just a cold," she said. But it was nice to have him going through the familiar routine, taking a thermometer out of its case, shaking it down, putting it under her tongue, taking her pulse, feeling her forehead.

He held up the thermometer and squinted at it. "101," he said. "Had any chills?" He nodded when she said yes. He got a throat stick from his little black bag and put it on her tongue. "Say 'ah'." He got out the stethoscope and she shivered as he put the cold steel ring on her chest. "Breathe in . . . and out . . . in . . . and out . . ." He took the ear plugs out of his ears, folded up the stethoscope neatly and put it back in its case.

"Lungs are clear. Throat's a little scrapey." He held a little light to her nose. "A little congested." He pushed her gently back under the covers. "Might be a touch of the grippe. Stay in bed till your fever goes down and stays down for at least half a day. Eat lightly. Drink a lot of liquids." He shook out some tablets onto the table. "Two every four hours till that achey feeling goes away."

"Could I have got it plane spotting this morning?" She explained about her stint on the roof.

"I'd be inclined to say not. Nobody knows too much about colds and grippe and flu, but my own theory is it comes from contact with somebody who's got it, not from getting your toes cold."

"Will you tell my mother that? She's threatening to keep me from plane spotting any more."

"Sure, I'll tell her." He sat back and smiled at her. "Mrs. Winslow wants to know why you haven't been by to see her."

"I was afraid she might be too busy. . . ."

"She'd enjoy seeing you. She gets awful lonesome for Jed." He sighed, put his head back and closed his eyes.

"You look tired," she said.

"Yeah. A mite weary. I miss young Lloyd."

The other general practitioner in town, Dr. Lloyd

Mason, had enlisted in the Army, to everyone's surprise. He was a good doctor but he was a rather frail, reserved young man, who had not seemed the type to rush off and enlist.

"Have you heard from him?"

"Not since he was in Officers' Training at Fort Dix, but I ran into Beatrice Patton up in Hamilton the other day, and she said he's been assigned to Patton's outfit, First Armored Division. They're out in the California desert somewhere, on maneuvers." He smiled. "That's a combination, isn't it? Young Lloyd, and tough old George."

"Yes. I watched Major Patton play polo in Hamilton once. I'd hate to have him mad at me."

"Me too." He got up and stretched. "I suppose my kid will go and sign himself up one of these days."

"Jed?" The idea startled her. "Not when he's just started college."

"A lot of 'em are. They see it as the more pressing need, I guess." He shook his head. "We should have nailed that whole mess down back there in Spain."

"*No pasarán,*" Elinor said.

"What's that?"

"Jed wrote that under the news clipping about the boy from Brooklyn who died with the Lincoln Brigade."

"That's right. Has it on his wall, doesn't he. *No pasarán.* Well, unfortunately they did pass." He picked up his black bag. "But maybe the English and the Yanks can change that." He stared thoughtfully at the darkened window. "And a lot of other brave people. Well, Ellie, take care of yourself and call me if you don't feel better in the morning." He turned back. "And I'll tell

71

your mother it wasn't the plane spotting." He winked at her and went down the stairs.

Elinor took two of the tablets he had left, lay back and closed her eyes. Tom in the Army Ski Patrol. Maybe Jed in something soon. It was all very upsetting. She picked up the cold washcloth her mother had brought her and put it over her eyes, although it was no longer cold. She wished when she woke up in the morning, the war would be over.

CHAPTER ELEVEN

It was a miserable week. She had to stay home with
her cold until Thursday, so she had a lot of work to
make up. And her mother was very upset about Tom's
enlistment. She felt betrayed because he had enlisted first
and told her afterward. She kept bursting into tears
at unexpected moments and saying, "He'll be killed," until Elinor felt as if her own nerves were stretched out
like thin wires.

"It's your father's fault," she kept saying to Elinor.
"He's always going on how we have to stop fascism.
Tom's been just drinking it in."

"Well, don't we?" Elinor said, exasperated. "Isn't that what your knitting for Britain is all about?"

"Of course not," her mother said. "That's just humanitarian. Those people are cold."

"I suppose people are cold in Germany, too," Elinor said.

Her mother gaver her a withering look. "You don't make sense, Elinor. In the first place, we can't send things to Germany."

She was right, of course. So often people whom Elinor felt in her bones were wrong came up with logical sounding arguments. She hated to argue.

And then in school on Friday she got into a stupid discussion in English class with a girl she couldn't stand. The girl had read a theme of her own on the subject of Father Coughlin, whom she admired. Elinor, remembering her father's and Tom's rage as they listened to the anti-Semitic, anti-labor, anti-New Deal tirades of the Detroit priest on the radio every week, took issue with the girl.

"He's like Hitler," she said. "He wants to destroy the Jews and have fascism here."

"What's wrong with that?" the girl said.

For a moment Elinor was too shocked to answer. Then she made the longest speech she had made in a class that year, about the evils of fascism, the un-Christian horror of persecuting Jews.

The girl interrupted her, finally. "I just think that since you have to take all your information from hearsay and you can't check out anything for yourself. . . ."

She in turn was interrupted. Miss Jones banged the flat of her hand on her desk and her eyes blazed.

"That's enough, Miss Evans! If you can't discuss a topic with calmness and courtesy, then I'll have to ask you to keep still."

The girl glared at Miss Jones, but she didn't have enough nerve to talk back.

Miss Jones, still angry, looked around the room. "I want this made clear right now. There will be no personal remarks in my class. Do you all understand that?"

Some of them nodded; some looked at their desks in embarrassment. For the rest of the period Elinor kept silent, trying to avoid looking at anyone. She was thinking that she would speak to her father again about dropping out of this ridiculous post-graduate year.

After class a boy she had never noticed much caught up with her in the hall. "That Miriam is a real jerk," he said. "Everybody knows that. She's got a brain the size of a Mexican jumping bean."

Elinor looked at him. He was a year younger and considerably smaller than most of the boys in his class. Elinor vaguely remembered hearing that he was very bright, especially in science. She didn't know what to say to him, so she just said, "Is that right?"

"Sure," he said. "Nobody has any respect for her."

She laughed. "Well, they're not exactly staggering under a load of respect for me, either. Most of them don't even speak to me." It surprised her that she had made such an admission to a stranger.

"You don't give them a chance," he said. "They're scared of you."

She looked at him in astonishment. "Scared of me? Why?"

Well, you're older and all that." He grinned suddenly. "You're one of the 'big kids.' Besides, you're the doctor's daughter."

"What's that got to do with it?"

"I don't know. Something about prestige. No, respect, I guess. Most of us have been dragged into the world by Dr. Winslow and your father, and we've had 'em hovering over us when we had our tonsils out and all that. Doctors are like gods, in a way. Or that's how it looks. They can save your life, or not."

The boy turned off to another corridor. Elinor watched his small, slight figure go quickly away until he was out of sight. It was odd that he had spoken to her like that. She shrugged and went along to her chemistry class.

Later when she was in the drugstore having a Moxie, a boy who had been in her graduating class came in. He was in Navy uniform.

"Ben!" she said.

"Hi, Ellie." He came over and sat down opposite her. "Long time no see."

"I didn't know you'd joined up."

"Yep. I figured Uncle Sam needed me." He grinned and shoved his white cap onto the back of his head.

"What's it like?" She really wanted to know. What young men did in the services seemed mysterious to her, and now that her brother and perhaps Jed would soon be involved, she wanted very much to know.

But Ben laughed and shrugged. "It ain't so bad. You swab a lot of decks, say 'yessir' a whole lot."

"Have you been to sea?"

He grew serious. "Can't talk about it, Ellie."

"Oh, sure. I shouldn't have asked." She thought of the rumors of U.S. ships carrying lend-lease to England being torpedoed and sunk by German U-boats. It awed her to think of Ben Barker defending American shipping. Ben Barker, a terrible English student, almost as bad as she was, but pretty good at math, and very good at first base. A good dancer. A nice kid she'd known all her life. "Take care of yourself, Ben," she said impulsively, as he got up to shake hands with Mr. Conolly.

"Don't you worry. Old Seaman Barker's got a good witch ridin' with him."

Elinor felt envious. Ben seemed more grown-up, jaunty, sure of himself. She wished she could just clear out and join something. But what could girls do? She wondered if she were old enough to join the Red Cross. Or if they'd take somebody that could hardly read or write.

Ben called to her when she was leaving. "Want to go to a show tonight? They're playing *Gone with the Wind* at the Ware."

"Sure. I'd love to." She went out feeling better. She'd already seen *Gone with the Wind* twice, but that didn't matter. She often went to her favorite movies three or four times. And she felt proud to be going out with a Navy man. Ben had never dated her before. She knew most of the girls he used to date were away at college, but never mind. "Count your blessings," as her mother often said but seldom did.

When she got home, her mother told her that the Winthrops had invited them for Thanksgiving dinner. That was a relief. Elinor had been worried about Thanksgiving without her father. He had always made a lot of Thanksgiving and Christmas. Now they would be in someone else's house and it would all be different. That would be better.

"Is Jed coming home?"

"I presume so," her mother said. "His mother didn't say."

That night Jed called her, just before Ben came to pick her up. "Hey," he said, "I hear you're coming to dinner on Turkey Day."

"Yes. Are you coming home?"

"You bet. And I've got some news."

She tried to get him to tell her what it was, but he just said, "Sit tight. I'll tell you when I see you."

Before the showing of *Gone with the Wind* that evening, there was a newsreel that showed pictures of the terrible devastation in England. Elinor shivered, imagining what it must be like to live in a state of constant danger and destruction. She tried to read the faces of the English people jammed together on the steps leading down to a subway station used as an air raid shelter, people for whom there was no room.

Ben held her hand and chewed gum solemnly throughout the newsreel, then relaxed and seemed to enjoy the feature film.

Later they sat for a long time in the Sentimental Shop, a Greek ice cream and candy shop that high school students frequented.

"That was a great picture," Ben said, attacking the piled up scoops of ice cream topped with whipped cream and a cherry.

"Yes, I love it." Elinor felt dreamy. "It was a terrible war too, but somehow it seems so different from now. I mean it was more all in one place. You knew it wouldn't explode all around you."

Mistaking her feeling for fear, Ben put his hand protectively over hers. "Don't you worry. We'll be in soon,

78

and the Yanks will end this thing in a hurry. Nothing's going to explode around you, Ellie."

"Don't you feel, though, all the time as if something's about to happen?" She laughed apologetically. "Of course it *is* happening. But I mean . . . something unimaginable. Like the world is spinning faster and faster, and it may go hurtling right off its axis."

"Listen, don't you worry. Things are kind of crazy right now, that's the truth. But they'll get straightened out. We're going to whip hell out of those guys, and then everything will settle down just like it used to be. I'll be back working at Sears, Roebuck, going out with pretty girls, and eating rainbow sundaes every day in the week if I want." He meant to sound reassuring, but for a moment he looked frightened, as if he didn't believe his own words.

It was Elinor's turn to be comforting. "Sure you will, Ben. And darned soon, I'll bet." But she had a sudden conviction that she would never see him again; and at that moment she felt almost painfully fond of him.

CHAPTER TWELVE

Elinor felt too wide awake to sleep after her evening with Ben. She lay curled up in bed with the radio playing softly so her mother wouldn't hear it.

When she and Ben had arrived at her front porch, he had kissed her, more fervently than she had been kissed before. She found herself enjoying it; but at the same time in the back of her mind she knew she was thinking of Ben not as the boy she had always known, but as a U.S. Navy man, a potential war hero. Maybe it didn't make any difference. Jed said she analyzed her reactions too much, and perhaps he was right.

While he was kissing her, Ben took off his cap and shoved it into his jacket pocket. Elinor touched his very short, curly blond hair and thought it felt "crisp." That was a funny word for hair, she thought; maybe "springy" was what she meant. He held her tight, but his bulky Navy pea jacket was uncomfortable.

The light in the front hall went on, and Ben jumped back. He muttered something about calling her later and was gone before she had time to say good night. She was annoyed. Her mother had a gift for making people feel guilty when there was no need for it. She pulled open the door and went in.

Her mother, in her housecoat, had gone back into the living room. "Bring the young man inside," she said. "I'll go upstairs. You can't stand out there catching more cold."

"He's gone. You scared him off."

"Oh?" Her mother was counting through a deck of new cards. "What was he afraid of?" She gave Elinor a sharp glance.

"People's mothers don't usually spring up and turn on all the lights when a boy is saying good night to a girl."

"It takes two seconds to say good night," her mother said. "Possibly six more for you to say 'thank you for a nice evening.' And surely lights are normal after dark."

"Oh, Mother." Elinor turned away. What good was it to argue.

"Did you have a nice evening?" Her mother chose to ignore Elinor's irritation.

"Yes, if you really want to know, I did."

"The boy is in the Navy?"

"Yes."

"Well, I suppose he'll be stationed at Great Lakes. That's where they train them."

"Mother, he's been trained. He's already been through the Great Lakes station."

"Oh, I see. Why are you so belligerent?"

"I'm not."

"Of course you are. You're very cross lately. I think it's that new teacher, the one you do that ridiculous plane spotting with. She's a bad influence."

Elinor gritted her teeth. All her life her mother had blamed whatever she disliked about Elinor's behavior on a friend. The accusations always offended Elinor. "That doesn't make sense," she said.

Her mother shrugged and put the cards down on the table with a little slap. "Your father called. He wants you to come to Boston tomorrow."

Elinor was surprised out of her anger. "He called me?"

"Well, he certainly didn't call to talk to me," her mother said drily.

"But I plane spot tomorrow."

"He knows that. He wants you to come up on the three-forty train. He'll meet you at North Station. Take your overnight things." She turned away. "I'm having an International Tea here tomorrow. The Women's Club. Try not to mess up the house."

Elinor started up the stairs. "What's an International Tea?"

"Each person represents a nation. It's to raise money for the Red Cross."

The ways in which her mother's clubs raised money for their various projects always baffled Elinor. They put on elaborate teas and bridge parties and charged themselves for coming. It seemed simpler just to donate the the cash. Her father told her she didn't understand the clubwoman mentality. "They wouldn't give if they didn't have a chance to get together and shriek and gossip."

As she lay in bed dreamily listening to Tommy Dorsey on the radio, she thought about her inability to understand her mother and the other women. I must be a nut, she thought. I'll never fit in. Maybe it's because I got hit on the head.

When her alarm went off early in the morning, she found she had gone to sleep with the radio on. Some one was reading the weather report. ". . . high clouds. Winds moderate out of the southeast, from Block Island to Sandy Hook. No precipitation expected before Monday morning."

That was good. She could do without precipitation up on the school roof. She wondered if it was cold out. She tried to peer out the window, but it was still pitch dark with a faint streak of light up high where the stars should be.

As she dressed, she thought of something Ben had said. He'd promised, kiddingly, to send her a postcard every time he knocked off a German. She'd answered that she hadn't thought of the Navy as knocking off people, especially when war hadn't been declared.

"Oh, it's just a matter of weeks," he'd said. "We'll be in it up to our ears." He'd looked pleased and excited. "And this little old boy is going to be right in there." He pantomimed firing in a wide circle with a machine gun. At least that was what she had thought. But from other things he said, it suddenly occurred to her that he was stationed on a submarine. It was a frightening idea.

She knew better than to mention it, but it stayed in her mind, worrying her. The idea of Ben scurrying along the bottom of the ocean in a tin trap, "a sardine can" as they were called sometimes, was scary. And killing people. She hadn't yet been able to picture any of the boys she knew, Ben or Tom or Jed or any of the others in town, going out and killing other people. You grew up thinking it was wrong to kill. What made it suddenly all right, just because somebody said, "There's a war on"? It troubled her.

She ate a hasty breakfast and rode her bike along the slippery, frosted street. Miss Jones's little car was already at the school.

The big front door was unlocked. It was dark in the school except for an occasional light along the corridor. A school all silent and dark was an eerie place, especially when it was a school you had gone to. She glanced into the room where she had been in the fourth grade. It was changed around now, made into a first grade room, so it didn't even look the same. She wondered if anybody remembered that she'd always been the first with answers in history and geography, that she'd written a short story that was published in the school's mimeographed magazine. Before that golf ball came sailing out of nowhere to knock her life into a jumble of confusion and embarrassment.

And yet she realized that she hadn't been as upset yesterday when what's-her-name made those snide remarks, as she used to be when people were mean about her inability to read and write properly. Maybe she was getting resigned. Or maybe, she thought, as she began to climb the stairs to the roof, other things had begun to seem more important than her personal problems. How could you use up all your energy grieving over the fact that people thought you were stupid, when in so many parts of the world people were dying from bombs and other people were losing their homes and their families? She wondered if it hurt when you were hit by a bomb or if you were dead before you knew what hit you.

She stepped through the trapdoor onto the roof. Miss Jones, bundled up again in her old raccoon coat, was standing by the roof ledge, studying the dark sky. She turned quickly.

"Am I late?" Elinor asked.

"No, I was early. I couldn't sleep."

"Boy, I could!" Elinor said. "I'm still sleepy."

"I saw you at the movies last night."

"Oh, did you?" It surprised her, for some reason, that Miss Jones went to movies. "Did you like the show?"

Miss Jones shrugged. "I'm not romantic enough, I guess. And I've never been amused by willful women."

Elinor didn't know what to say to that so she said nothing. She went into the shack to sign in. "That chart you gave me was a big help," she called out to Miss Jones. "It really helped me to learn which is which." She looked at the much bigger chart hanging on the wall. She noticed a plane that hadn't been on her chart. "What's the name of this new one?" she asked. The name was underneath, but she didn't trust herself not to reverse digits.

"CG-13. It's a troop glider."

"Oh." Elinor studied it. "Does it land troops, do you think? Like an airborne truck or something?"

"Yes." Miss Jones was watching her now. "We never

did get together to try having you touch words, did we?"

"I don't think it will work." They went outside to watch the sky.

"How do you spell 'valiant'?"

"Valiant? V. .a. . ." She hesitated. She didn't want to do this now. She knew she couldn't spell "valiant," and Miss Jones knew it. Why was she pestering her with that? She felt angry. "I don't know."

"Try it."

They stood together at the end of the roof, each of them staring off in different directions. It was odd to talk to someone when neither person looked at the other one.

"What comes after v-a-?" Miss Jones was persistent.

"Oh, I don't know." Then in a rush she said, "l-i-t-n."

"Go into the shack and trace the word 'valiant,' " Miss Jones said. "It's under that BT-13 silhouette. . . ."

Elinor interrupted. "I know what plane it is. Why do I need to spell it?"

"Try it. Please. Trace the word and then come back out."

Disgruntled, Elinor went into the shack. She hadn't come up here to be badgered about her spelling. Miss Jones meant well, but she ought to leave school stuff for school. Quickly Elinor located the stubby silhouette of the BT-13, and with her forefinger she traced the letters of its name, Valiant.

"Now spell it for me," Miss Jones said.

Elinor sighed. She'd just get it all mixed up again. "V-a-l-i-a-n-t," she said rapidly, hoping Miss Jones would accept this failure and leave her alone. Next to the people who made fun of her, the worst ones were those who were determined to help her.

"Elinor!"

Elinor turned her head. Miss Jones was looking at her with delight. "It worked!"

"What worked?"

"You spelled it right! Somehow tracing the letters with your finger makes them register in your brain. Some people learn by hearing, some by seeing. You learn by touch. Elinor, this is marvelous!"

The little stir of hope inside her made Elinor doubly wary. She'd been through too many experiments, too many theories, that hadn't worked out. "It was probably luck," she said. "I suppose just by the law of averages I'm bound to get a word right sometimes."

"I don't think so. I don't think so. I think we've hit on something . . ."

Elinor held up her hand. "Wait a sec." She cocked her head, listening intently. "There's a plane, coming in from the west. . . . Sounds like a single engine, small plane. Maybe just a Piper Cub, but . . ." She held her binoculars to her eyes, trying in vain to penetrate the dark gray veil of the predawn sky. "I'd better phone it in."

She called it in, trying to visualize in her mind the command post in Boston where Army men plotted every reported plane on a huge map. She wished she could see that room sometime.

After the sun came up and the clouds lifted, she and Miss Jones were busy. Many planes were up today, including all the bothersome little single-engine training planes from the local airport. They had to be reported like everything else. It seemed as if suddenly everyone was learning to fly.

Time after time Elinor saw planes or heard them before Miss Jones did. Once all she saw was a flash of silver very high in the sky as the sun touched the wing of a plane. She watched tensely, thinking of stories of how fighter pilots like to fly with the sun behind them so the enemy couldn't see to shoot at them. This one turned out to be a big bomber, a B-17 Flying Fortress with its four engines. It was the first one Elinor had reported, or indeed seen. She was excited about calling it in. Afterward she watched its progress until it was out of sight in the south. Someone else would be calling it in now. It was nice to feel part of a system that protected the coast. Her mother scoffed at the idea that enemy planes would ever be sighted here, but that was whistling in the dark. It could happen. Hitler had a way of making war first and announcing it later. And he was very angry with the Americans for all their help to the English.

Because they were so busy, the time flew by, and they had no chance to talk any more about Elinor's ability, or lack of it, to remember words from tracing. It was not until she was on the train going to Boston that afternoon that she thought of it again. She tried to think what it would mean if it were true. It would be like learning to read from scratch. She'd have to trace every word and learn it as if she were in the first grade learning to read by sight. It sounded like a stupendous job. But it might be worth it. She was unwilling to get her hopes up, however. She had heard enough about the brain to know that cells destroyed could never be renewed. She didn't know if cells *had* been destroyed in her brain. People didn't seem to know much about the brain yet.

She got a cinder in her eye, and by the time she got it out, the train was pulling into the big smoky, sooty North Station that always smelled like gas. When she saw her father waiting for her at the gate, she broke into a run and threw herself into his arms. She hadn't quite realized how much she had missed him. He kept his arm around her as he led her out to the car.

He seemed as happy as she was. "We're going to have a weekend to end all weekends," he said. "I've got tickets for *The Little Foxes,* and we're going to dinner at the Copley Plaza, and we are going to have ourselves a man-sized ball!"

Elinor squeezed his arm. "Oh, I wish I could live with you all the time."

"Honey," he said, "bless your heart." He opened the car door for her, but he didn't say, "Why don't you come and live with me?"

She loved his small Beacon Street apartment, partway up the hill. It had a view of the golden dome of the State House and of the Common. At the back of the third-floor walk-up there was a small iron balcony overlooking a garden, which would be pretty in the spring. At the moment its main interest was the bird bath and the bird feeders. Elinor's father pointed out a fat robin, "too lazy to go south."

Her father had furnished the apartment simply, with some antiques bought from shops on Charles Street, and a few comfortable modern chairs, two of them pulled up to the small fireplace.

He ushered her into the tiny guest room and left her to unpack her things and wash off the soot from the train. After a quick shower she put on the new robe that her mother had just given her for her birthday, and went out to the living room. She didn't want to dress for dinner yet. "Do you mind?" she asked him. "I'll get all mussed if I dress now."

"Of course not. You have a new robe. Birthday?"

She nodded.

He lit his pipe and looked at her through the curling smoke. "I haven't given you your present yet."

"That's all right."

"I didn't forget it. I have it." He tapped the pocket of his jacket. "Did you have a party?"

"No. Mother said I could, but who would come? Everybody I like is somewhere else."

"Yes. It seems to be that kind of time." He sat down in a low leather chair, stretching his legs out in front of him. "Tommy's going to have brunch with us tomorrow."

"Oh, good! That's a good birthday present all by itself. He called me on my birthday. He'll be leaving for officers' training next week."

"Yes. They don't lose any time nowadays. Once you sign on, you're scooped up so fast, you don't know what hit you." He poked at the bowl of his pipe with a wooden match. "I tried to enlist."

She was startled. "*You* did?"

He gave her a wry smile. "Did you think I was too old?"

"No, of course not. . . . You just surprised me."

"Well, I am too old. That and the fact that the hospital allegedly needs me. I was turned down."

She didn't know what to say. "I'm sorry if you're disappointed, but I . . . I'd be scared spitless if you went too. It's bad enough with Tommy and the others . . ."

"I know. Well, don't worry about Tom. He has a way of landing on his feet like a smart cat." He jumped up quickly as the doorbell rang. "I asked someone to come by and meet you. . . ."

"I'm not dressed!" She started to get up but he waved her back.

"You look fine. No need to be formal."

She couldn't imagine who it was. Usually he *was* rather formal, or at least conventional, with other people. Listening intently she heard an unfamiliar woman's voice greeting him. For a moment she thought of her mother's accusations about "some woman" in Boston, but she put it out of her mind at once.

He came in, opening the door for a young woman of about thirty. The two things that struck Elinor first were how happy and almost boyish he looked, and how attractive and foreign-looking the young woman was. She was tall and slim, with dark hair worn in a braid around her head. She had searching dark eyes, and a certain tightness in her mouth.

"Elsa," Elinor's father said, "this is my daughter Elinor. Elinor, this is Frau Elsa Braun."

Embarrassed and little irked with her father for letting her be caught in her robe, she stood up and said, "How do you do. I'm sorry I'm not dressed."

Frau Braun shook hands with her, a firm single shake, and said, "It is no matter. How do you do. I am pleased to meet you." She looked at Elinor appraisingly, but she didn't smile.

"Let me take your coat, Elsa," Elinor's father said. "Do

sit down and I'll light the fire. Would you like sherry?"
He seemed rattled.

Elinor waited politely until Frau Braun had made herself comfortable. She had never seen her father nervous like that. He was always so self-possessed. She couldn't understand how he happened to know a German woman. It was very peculiar.

The visit did not go well. Elinor's father poured the sherry and brought out a plate of tiny, delicious cookies from S.S. Pierce. He tried to be sparkling and amusing. Elinor tried to be polite. But for some reason she was filled with dread.

Frau Braun certainly had a charm of her own, an acerbic wit that came out in tiny explosions when you least expected it. It was a wit tinged with bitterness that also made you uncomfortable. She was not good at small talk. When she asked a question, it was because she wanted to hear the answer. She seemed to Elinor to be a person who had stripped away all the usual social superfluities, either because it was her temperament to do so or because she had been forced to. It was impossible to imagine her, for instance, at one of Elinor's mother's teas. She could imagine the expression on Frau Braun's face if she walked in on the scene Elinor had briefly witnessed in her house just before she left to take the train: two dozen women dressed in their own notion of what an Indonesian or a Japanese or a Jordanian woman would wear—two dozen different countries represented, except that there had been a slipup resulting in Mrs. Gray and Mrs. Petersham both coming as Brazilians. Mrs. Gray had just arrived when Elinor came downstairs, and the shrieks of glee and derision had been deafening. Mrs. Gray and Mrs. Petersham were making huge efforts to be good sports and laugh it off, but the indignation of each with what she considered the other's error was visible. Elinor had left hastily.

Frau Braun would never be ridiculous or pathetic, Elinor felt quite sure. She wondered if she would go on being called "Frau." It didn't seem like a good idea, with anti-German sentiment so strong. What *was* the woman doing here? How did her father know her? And why was he so nervous, so eager to please? She felt a little faint in her stomach, anticipating some unknown disaster.

Nobody referred to Frau Braun's background and Elinor thought it would be rude to ask. But when Frau Braun asked Elinor what courses she was taking, she said, "In my country the course of study at your age is more rigorous." Elinor felt vaguely apologetic as if she were responsible for America's laxity in its schools. Then immediately afterward she felt defensive.

"I think you can learn quite a lot in our schools if you really want to," she said, "and if you're . . . up to it." She was sorry she'd gotten into that. But Frau Braun simply looked at her with her beautiful eyebrows slightly arched in skepticism.

Frau Braun stayed so long that Elinor had to hurry to get dressed for dinner. There was no real conversation with her father until they were finally seated at their table in the dining room at the Copley Plaza.

After he had ordered for them both, he said, "How did you like Elsa?" He asked it very casually, busying himself with trying the martini that the wine steward had brought him.

93

"She's very attractive," Elinor said. "Very intelligent."

He drank half the martini. "But you didn't like her."

He looked so bleak, she hastened to reassure him. "I didn't see her long enough to know. You know me, Dad—I'm the slow reactor."

He didn't smile. After a long silence he said, "You're wondering about her, I suppose. Where she comes from and all that."

"Well, I did wonder."

Speaking slowly he said, "She's a German refugee."

"Oh. Jewish?"

"No, although her husband was a Jew." He spoke without looking at her, frowning into his glass, as if the subject were painful. "Her husband and she were physicists. He was shot—she saw him shot down in cold blood."

Elinor shivered. "How terrible."

"Yes." He waited while the busboy brought celery and olives and small sesame-seed crackers. "She had a miraculous escape herself, through friends, a little like the Underground Railroad in this country before the Civil War, one person passed her on to the next." He took a quick breath and looked at Elinor. "So now she is here. Safe, I hope."

Elinor salted a piece of celery and bit into it. She was trying to revise her impression of Frau Braun. "She shouldn't be called 'Frau,' " she said. "Too many people hate Germans now."

"You're right. I try to remember. Only it seems insulting, somehow, to call her Mrs. Brown. As if she's lost her identity."

"I suppose she has, in a way."

He smiled for a moment. "No. Elsa will never lose her identity. No matter what they her...Snow White or Mrs. Abercrombie or ..."

As he paused, Elinor said, "Or Brunhilde."

He looked surprised, and then he laughed. "She *is* a bit Brunhildian, isn't she. Although she's not blonde, and she is not a warrior and she wouldn't conspire to murder her lovers."

"No, of course not. I just meant...she looks like a German queen or something." She laughed uncomfortably, sorry she'd started this. "Not that I know many German queens."

He was looking off across the candle-lit room, thoughtfully. "It's the dignity, I think. The regalness. It struck me too when I first met her."

Elinor longed to talk about something else. She felt as if she were skating on Ricker's pond, as she used to do when she was younger, going fast and seeing how close she could get to the thin black ice. You could hear the ominous crackle and see the shooting lines in the ice....

"Oh, good," she said. "Here's the soup."

CHAPTER THIRTEEN

They waited in the lobby of the Parker House for Tom.

"He's late," Elinor said. "Maybe something happened."

"He'd have called. Don't be such a worrier, Ellie. It's a waste of energy."

Elinor didn't try to explain that she had no control over her tendency to worry. She peered out across the Common, looking for Tom's familiar quick stride. It was an overcast day, and in spite of the Weather Bureau's assurances, it had begun to snow a little. She wondered if Jed had gone skiing. He'd told her about the great skiing at Hanover and the new J-bar.

She came back to her father. He was sitting in a big

chair reading a copy of the *Boston Transcript* that somebody had left behind. "Should we call him up?"

"Relax, dear. He's only a few minutes late. The subway is irregular on Sundays."

"I thought he would drive in."

"He's sold his car."

"Oh." She wished he hadn't. She could have looked
after it for him. That car was his pride and joy. "I could
have taken care of it."

"He got a good price for it. Now that they aren't
making any more cars, the prices are up."

Someone tapped her shoulder. She whirled around.
Tom stood there smiling, in uniform. It hadn't occurred
to her that he would be in uniform. It made his enlistment more real than it had been before. "Tom!" she
said. "You look beautiful!"

"How do you like it?" Tom shook hands with his
father. "I got it at Brooks Brothers. Might as well fight
this war in style."

"Do you have to buy your own?" Elinor said.

"Officers do. Enlisted men get outfitted. I understand
the things never fit. Are we going to eat here? I'm
starved. I've been packing since seven o'clock. Nothing
but coffee in my poor emaciated body." With an arm
around each of them he took them into the dining room.
"Are you paying, Dad?"

"Sure."

"Good. I didn't bring any money."

They sat down and ordered. Both of the men shuddered when Elinor ordered Parker House rolls and tripe.

"Tripe for breakfast?" Tom said.

"It's almost noon. And it's their specialty. I believe in
ordering specialties." She couldn't stop looking at Tom.

He looked so handsome and so adult. It awed her. She listened to him talk with a feeling that he was a stranger she had just met. He would be at officers' training camp for ninety days, he told them, and then he would probably be shipped to Washington state.

"So far?" she said.

"You don't join up to stay at home," he said. He looked at his father. "How's Elsa?"

Elinor felt a stab of jealousy. He knew Elsa, then. He knew all about whatever there was to know.

"Fine. She found a place to live in Brookline. She'll be looking for a job."

Tom looked serious. "She may have trouble, you know."

"I know. She knows. It's so stupid. She's a good physicist. We need people like that. "

"But Roosevelt's got a blind spot about aliens. They say he tried to pressure Attorney General Biddle into interning all German aliens, but Biddle won't do it."

"There could be spies, couldn't there?" Elinor asked.

Her father frowned. "Of course there could. But when a person comes as well vouched for as Elsa . . ."

"I suppose a spy would take care to be vouched for." As her father shot a questioning look, she added, "I mean, you can see why they have to be careful."

"Well, my dear, Elsa is not a spy."

"Oh, of course not. I didn't mean that." But she wondered if she had half meant it. Maybe she wanted Elsa to be a spy or anything bad.

"She'd better not be." Tom smiled at his father. "Not if I see which way the wind is blowing."

Her father glanced at Elinor and gave Tom a little frown.

"You don't have to be cautious in front of me," Elinor said. "I'm not a child any more." She felt angry at being shut out.

Her father gave her a long look. "All right. You've got a point. I'm in love with her."

Elinor was sorry she had asked to be told. Now that he was saying it, she didn't want to hear it.

"But your mother swears she'll never give me a divorce. And anyway, in this state, a person can't remarry until five years after the divorce is final. God, I'll be an old man."

He looked so depressed, Elinor felt sorry for him. She forgot to be angry, although the whole situation seemed to her very unfortunate, if, she thought, that was the right word. She didn't know what to say.

"Live with her," Tom said.

Elinor gasped. "Tom!"

"Why not? These are troubled times, to coin a phrase. Why should peoople who love each other sacrifice everything because of a legal quibble?"

"Is that all marriage is, a legal quibble?" Elinor said. She was shocked at Tom's suggestion.

"You're only upset because it's Dad," Tom said. "You're not all that big a believer in marriage. At least I don't think you are. And if you are, you're crazy, because you can see the damage it's done in our family."

"You'd better not ever get to be a judge," she said.

"I probably won't," he said quietly.

His father grabbed his arm. "Come on! Cut it out. I asked you fellers out to breakfast to have a happy time. Cut out the gloom, will you?"

Tom grinned at him. "Sorry, Doc." He leaned back

as the waiter put the platter of tripe in front of Elinor. "Happy tripe, Sis."

She tried to laugh. She had learned a long time ago that when things got bad, you might as well laugh. But it was especially difficult today. "By the way," she said, "Miss Jones thinks I can learn to read by tracing the letters."

Her father put his fork down and stared at her. "She does? What makes her think so?"

"Oh, because I memorize silhouettes of airplanes by tracing them with my fingers. You know, it fixes the shape in my mind."

Her father looked at Tom. "Good God! Why didn't I ever think of that? Learning kinesthetically. . . . She might be right."

"Is it possible?" Tom said.

"We can train our minds in all sorts of ways that we usually don't." He jumped up and got a menu from the waiter. "Ellie, trace this word." He pointed to a word on the menu.

"Right now? I want to eat my tripe while it's hot." She wished her father didn't get so carried away with things. It was almost certainly not going to work. She'd just said it to change the subject. But when he insisted, she traced the word he was pointing to. She frowned and shook her head. "I'm not getting it. It doesn't make sense."

"What did you get?"

"P-u-l-l-e-r."

"You almost got it. It's butter. You confused the b for p, and the t's for l's."

She laughed. "That's a fairly big confusion." She

wished he'd drop it. It would only raise his hopes and disappoint him.

"You need to practice the letters of the alphabet. Ellie, give it a try when you get home, will you? It might work."

"Sure, I'll try. But don't hope for a lot, Dad."

His eyes were shining. "Wouldn't that be great? I'll see what I can find out about kinesthetic learning. There must be something on it."

At least, she thought, I got his mind off Frau Braun for a minute. And what a spoiled brat I am for being jealous.

When their father had gone to pay the bill, Tom said, "What do you think about Dad and Elsa?"

"I hate it."

"Why? Lord, the man needs a break. He's put up with so much for so long."

"I just hate it, that's all. She scares me. And she's German."

He laughed. "What a bigot you are. She scares me too, but only because she's so brilliant. She's really fond of the old man. And he deserves a little of that, doesn't he?"

"Mother was fond of him, too."

"Oh, Mother . . . she's so bloody possessive. She wants to own everybody. Nobody wants to be owned." He looked at Elinor seriously. "You be careful about that after I'm gone. Keep yourself to yourself. Don't let her take you over."

"Don't worry, I won't," Elinor said, but she knew it wouldn't be easy to keep herself to herself.

After Tom left them, she had trouble not crying. They wouldn't see him again till Christmas and after that, maybe . . . she didn't let herself finish with "never." Her father drove her to the station and waited with her for the train.

"Cheer up, dear," he said. "Tom will be fine." He pulled an envelope out of his pocket. "This is your birthday present. You can open it on the train. I want it to be a secret between us. Don't use it foolishly, that's all I ask. Keep it for a real need." And as the trainman opened the gate, he said, "And I know you won't mention Elsa to your mother."

"Of course not." She was hurt that he had felt he had to ask her not to speak of it.

"I know you won't. Call me tomorrow. I want to hear more about this reading idea. You practice on it, honey." He walked with her to the last car and helped her on. "Don't sit in the smoker." It was a joke; he always said it, because she complained when she had to walk through the smelly smoking car.

As soon as she was settled on the hard green plush seat, she opened the envelope. Inside it was a check for five hundred dollars. She stared at it, finding it hard to believe. He had given her an allowance of thirty dollars a month for the last three years, but he had never given her any other money. She thought of his saying "keep it for a real need," and she wondered with some alarm what kind of need he thought she'd have. Perhaps it was his way of giving her some degree of independence, of warning her, as Tom had, not to let her life be taken over. Thoughtfully she put in her purse. She'd open a savings account at the bank.

The conductor outside her window looked at his watch, lifted his arm, and called "All aboard!" The engine began to chuff and the wheels turned as he swung up out of sight onto the platform. In a minute he came through the car taking tickets.

Elinor opened the theater program, trying to think about the play she had seen and enjoyed the night before. She looked at the picture of Tallulah Bankhead on the cover. I wish I were beautiful and talented, she thought. I wish I were a brilliant scientist or something. I wish I could read.

CHAPTER FOURTEEN

On Thanksgiving Day Elinor went over to Jed's house in the morning, partly to help his mother with the dinner and partly to see Jed, who had come in late the night before. She was at once eager and reluctant to hear his "news." She tried not to speculate about what it might be.

"Hi!" He came running down the front steps to meet her and gave her a quick hug and a kiss on the cheek. "Good to see you."

"Oh, me too," she said. "I mean, you know, me you too." She laughed, feeling happier than she had in a long time. Jed looked wonderful. It didn't seem that he could look older in such a short time, and yet he did. "You look like a college man."

"That's me. Jed the Frat-house Boy."

She laughed again, remembering years ago when Jed had read her Horatio Alger's book, *Jed the Poorhouse Boy.* "I'm glad you're home. What's your big news?" She hadn't meant to ask him but there it was.

Just outside the door he stopped and looked at her, sobering. "I'm not sure it's going to be. It looks like I flunked it."

"Flunked what?" She felt relieved, although she didn't know why.

"I thought I'd been accepted by the Army Air Corps. I passed all the tests. But when I went for my physical, I got so nervous, my heart speeded up. Tachycardia. I've always had it when I got nervous. There's nothing at all wrong with my heart—it's just a nervous reaction. But they turned me down."

"Oh, Jed!" She knew now that that was what she had been dreading, that he had joined one of the services. Because he looked so disappointed, she tried hard not to be glad he'd been turned down.

"I get one more chance. I think Dad can tell me how to lick it, but he won't. He's mad. He wants me to finish medical school."

"He's always had his heart set on your being a doctor."

"I know. Well, so have I, but things are different now. I tried to make him see. I've been classified 1-A, and I'll just be drafted for the stupid infantry if I wait." He opened the door, and they went inside.

"Ellie, dear," Jed's mother said. "How are you?" She had the partly cooked turkey on top of the stove, basting it. Her cheeks were flushed from the heat. "How pretty you look in that blouse." She put the cover back on the big enamel roaster. "Doesn't it smell good? Jed, will you lift it into the oven for me, dear?"

"What can I do to help?" Elinor said, admiring Mrs. Winthrop. She was a pretty woman, and her eyes were warm and sparkly as if she really liked you.

"Let's see . . ." Mrs. Winthrop washed her hands and dried them on a roller towel. "Perhaps you and Jed would like to set the table. The big white linen table-cloth, Jed, and the best silver." She laughed. "Twice a year I show off."

Jed's younger brother Cy was sitting on the dining room floor cracking nuts. "Hi, Ellie," he said. "What's new?" He looked like his mother, with an added touch of mischief in his eyes.

"There's a war on," Ellie said. That had become a popular saying at school. "There's a war on" or "Don't you know there's a war on?" whether it had anything to do with the subject or not.

"You're kidding me," he said. "What war? Civil? Of the Roses? Whiskey Rebellion?"

"Of the Roses," she said. "I'm a Roundhead. Who are you?"

"No, no, no," he said, "you're suffering from mistaken identity. You're Margaret of Anjou, that's who you are, and isn't that a red rose I see behind your ear?"

"Jeepers," Jed said, "I've got a prodigy for a kid brother."

"I'm a war buff," Cy said. He held out a shelled walnut to Elinor. "Walnut?"

"Thanks, Cy."

"You're going to have to move your warlike carcass," Jed said opening the drawers of the big buffet and getting out the folded linen tablecloth. "We aren't going to step over you."

"Ever obliging." Cy scooped up the unshelled nuts in the newspaper he had been using to hold them. "If you don't want me, my mother does."

"She's stuck with you," Jed called after him. And as Cy disappeared behind the swinging door, Jed shook his head. " 'War buff.' I guess the only people who think war is fun are the ones who haven't been in one."

"But you want to get in." Elinor helped him flip the big tablecloth over the table.

"Hold it," he said. "I forgot to put the leaves in the table." And as she gathered up the tablecloth and he got the wide mahogany leaves from the closet and fitted them into the pulled-out table he said, "You can't help getting a little excited, especially at this stage, when we aren't in it yet. But I don't expect it to be fun, I really don't. I used to be a war buff, too, at Cy's age, but I was too thorough. I read too many accounts and looked at too many pictures. Now we can put the tablecloth on. Anyway, it's just that I know I'm going to have to be in it, so I'd rather pick my own service. In a plane at least you don't see the people die. You don't run 'em through with a bayonet or mow them down with artillery fire. I know that doesn't make sense—the people a pilot or a bombardier kills are just as dead as anybody else. It's just that you don't have to face up to it quite as much. At least that's how it hits me."

She thought of Elsa Braun seeing her husband shot dead. She shivered.

Jed noticed and put his arm around her for a moment. "It must be rough to be a girl at a time like this. All you can do is watch and wait."

"Oh, that's not true," she said. "Most of the people in the defense factories now are women, and there's the Red Cross, and Civil Defense . . ." She broke off and laughed. "And don't forget, I am a valued member of the Army's Report Center Staff."

"What's that?"

"Plane spotting. And don't knock it, old boy. I nearly froze to death last Saturday."

He saluted. "If you do freeze to death, I'll personally see to it that you get the Purple Heart. With clusters." He handed her a lot of forks. "I never can remember which fork goes outside which. You'd better do it. I'll get the plates." He opened the door of the cupboard. "The Spode, I guess. Wouldn't you say she'd want the Spode?"

"Yes."

"I hear Tommy couldn't get away for Thanksgiving."

"No. He was disappointed."

"I wish I could ski as well as he can. I'd try to get into that outfit. He's a lucky duck."

"Ben Barker's in the Navy. He was home on leave."

Jed laughed. "No kidding. Old Ben. He's kind of big in the behind for those tight Navy pants."

"He looked very cute."

He shot a quick look at her. "Did he now?"

"I went out with him." She didn't like his making fun of Ben.

Lightly Jed said, "Better watch out. Those sailors learn a lot of tricks. A girl in every port, you know, all that stuff."

She started to answer indignantly but then it occurred to her that Jed was jealous. It was a flattering thought. A little coyly she said, "We had a very nice evening."

Jed didn't answer for a moment. He busied himself lifting down a stack of bread-and-butter plates. Then he said quietly, "Good for you." He put the plates on the table and went out into the kitchen.

Elinor caught the look on his face and knew she had hurt him. She felt ashamed of herself. She shouldn't pull that kind of stupid girly trick with Jed of all people. He was her dearest friend. Besides, it was the kind of behavior she'd always hated in other girls, all that phony trapping business.

When he came back carrying a tall cut glass vase full of roses, she said, "It wasn't all that great, the date with Ben. I mean it was nice but it wasn't fun like going out with you. We saw *Gone with the Wind*."

He looked cheered up. "Great Guns! How many times does that make that you've seen that thing?"

"Four, I think." She had seen it first with him.

"Why didn't he take you to something you hadn't seen?"

"He didn't know I'd seen it." And he didn't ask, she thought. Jed always consulted with her about what they would do on their dates. "Well, he's really a nice boy," she said, "but honest, I'd rather go out with you anytime."

Pleased, he tried to carry it off with a joke. "Natch. I'm known far and wide as the most exhilarating date in Essex County. Hey, do you put bread-and-butter plates here or here?"

She showed him where she thought they should go. "The roses are beautiful."

"Cy and I got them for Mother. They are pretty, aren't they?"

When they had finished with the table, and had helped wash up the cooking dishes for Mrs. Winslow, they whipped cream and beat egg whites for the eggnog that Dr. Winslow was making.

Later they were all sitting in the living room to rest for a few minutes, when Elinor's mother arrived. Mrs. Winslow jumped up to let her in.

"Claire, come in. I was just going to call and ask if Jed could come and get you so you wouldn't have to take the car out."

"Oh, that's all right. I didn't mind." Elinor's mother slipped out of her fur coat. "One has to be independent and resourceful and all that nowadays."

Elinor bit her lip. She hoped her mother wasn't going to be the abandoned faithful wife today, and make everybody uncomfortable.

But then her mother went on. "Thank you, Doctor," she said, as Dr. Winslow took her coat. "You're looking very well."

"You're the one who's looking well," Dr. Winslow said. "Splendid, Claire, splendid."

Her mother did look well, Elinor thought, as she came into the living room. She was wearing a becoming new purple wool dress, and she had had her hair done a little differently. Maybe it was a good sign. She held out her hands to Jed as he jumped up to greet her. She had always liked Jed.

"We've missed you," she said.

He smiled at her. "I'm glad. I love to be missed."

"Hello, Cy. My word, how you've grown in just a few months."

"Hello, Mrs. Golden. I'm planning to be a giant." He pulled up the most comfortable armchair. "Please sit down. I've been saving this chair just for you."

"It's probably booby-trapped with nutshells," Jed said. "Cy is in charge of shelling nuts, and he seems to be making it an all day job. It beats real work."

"Don't listen to him, Mrs. Golden," Cy said. He offered her some shelled nuts. "He's very crass."

She laughed and helped herself to nuts. It was the first time Elinor had heard her laugh in weeks. Maybe this was going to be a really good day after all.

CHAPTER FIFTEEN

Thanksgiving dinner was enjoyable. Elinor was proud of her mother for putting herself out to be charming and to act as if she had no troubles. Sometimes, she thought, watching her laugh at something Dr. Winslow had said, she really hated her mother, and at other times she loved her so much and felt so protective toward her, it literally hurt. Her mother had so many funny little vanities that made her vulnerable. She cared too much what people thought. She rebuilt reality to make it the way she wanted it, and then she believed her own version.

"Ellie, more of the good bird? More stuffing?" Dr. Winslow held out his hand for her plate.

She laughed and glanced at her mother. "Maybe just a little bit. It's so good."

After dinner Dr. Winslow and the boys and Elinor went for a walk. They cut across a vacant lot and down a side street until they came to the deserted beach.

Dr. Winslow squinted at the sky. "It's spitting snow," he said. "We'll get some real snow tonight."

They walked past the closed and shuttered hot dog stand and the popcorn booth and the place that sold seventeen kinds of ice cream.

"Nowadays when I look at a beach, I can't help picturing Germans swarming ashore," Jed said.

His father frowned. "Couldn't we just think about Pilgrims if we've got to think about that today? They swarmed ashore too."

"Unfortunately they aren't the guys who have their eye on us now," Jed said.

"I think you ought to tell Jed how to pass that Air Corps test, Dad," Cy said, looking unusually serious.

Dr. Winslow muttered something under his breath. He kicked at the densely packed wet sand with the toe of his storm boot. "You fellers go on ahead. I want to talk to Elinor a minute."

Jed gave him a searching look and then said, "All right, Cy, I'll race you to the cove." The two boys ran down the beach, sending up little showers of sand behind them.

Dr. Winslow turned his back to the wind and lit a cigar. He threw the match away with unnecessary vehemence. "You think I ought to help him get in, Ellie?"

"Oh, Dr. Winslow, I don't know. He's upset now, but he won't hold it against you if you don't . . ."

He interrupted her. "I don't give a hoot what he holds against me. Kids always hold it against you when you're trying to protect 'em. What I'm concerned with is, what's the right thing to do? I don't want him to go. I hate war. And he's too young. And we need good doctors. He'd be a good one. But where is the line between what I want for him and what is best for him?" He shoved his hat back on his head. "I'm blessed if I honestly know. He thinks he's grown-up . . . Do you feel grown-up?"

Elinor looked at his troubled face. "Oh, I don't know. Sometimes I do, but mostly I guess I don't quite. But I think Jed is."

"You do?"

"Yes. He's always had his head on the right way, as my dad says. He's always been more grown-up than a lot of the other kids."

He sighed. "I thought it was a stroke of fate when the Air Corps said no to him. And to be perfectly ethical, I ought to let it stand. But I know the boy's heart is sound as a drum. He's always had a tendency to tachycardia when he was all revved up about something. But I took him in for an EKG a couple of years ago, and Dr. Bliss gave him a real going-over. Not a sign of anything wrong. Just a nervous reaction."

"Would it interfere with his actions? I mean if he were flying and something happened?"

"No. The boy is sound as a dollar." He walked on slowly, looking down at the sand. Then he straightened up. "Well, I guess I have to do it. If he's a man, he's entitled to a man's decisions." He whistled, but the boys were too far ahead to hear him. "Besides, I'd hate myself if the kid got drafted and trapped in the trenches and blown up by some damned Nazi hand grenade." He looked at Elinor. "Your father told me about this kinesthetic business with your reading. Does it help any?"

"Yes, it does help some. But it's so slow."

"Well, Ellie, any progress is good."

"I know. I am getting to recognize some simple words. I often have to trace a word every time I come to it, though, and that takes so long. I guess I'll never settle down with *War and Peace*."

"I shouldn't wonder," he said, "if you could learn to do the tracing with your eye after a while."

"Really? I hadn't thought of trying that."

"Try it. I've been doing a lot of reading about this. Just lately some new things have come out. Not that they know much, but a lot of people are doing some educated guessing. Copying words down after you trace them might help."

"All right. I'll do that."

"And according to one feller I read, concentrate as hard as you can on sounds and get them equated in your mind with groups of letters. You know that old chestnut, '*i* before *e*, except after *c*' . . ."

" 'Or when sounded as *ay* in neighbor or weigh,' " she finished.

"Right. Well, think of the *ie* as a total sound, instead of two separate letters. Or *ough*, for instance. I think his idea is that you get to think of a common group of letters as one letter, and it's easier for you to remember it." He put his hand on her shoulder. "You're a good girl, Ellie. You've always had a lot of guts."

She was pleased, but in all honesty she felt he was wrong. "I get discouraged. I give up trying."

"As I understand it, that's part of what this damage

can do to you. Periods of depression, wanting to withdraw and shut out the whole bloomin' world, or the other way around—wanting to beat up on everybody."

"That's me."

"Well, when it gets rough, you come and see me and we'll crack a few jokes and go down to Conolly's for a Moxie."

"I really appreciate that," she said.

"And I mean it. I'm never too busy for you. 'Course sometimes you may have to grab me by the coattails, but you do it." He raised his arm and waved to the boys, who were walking back toward them. "They don't come back as fast as they took off. Jed's afraid of what I'm going to say." He chuckled. "Stubborn kid."

Jed began to talk about a dog they'd just seen down the beach, a basset hound. "Makes you bust out crying just to look at him," he said to Elinor. "Gad, what a mournful face." Then he faced his father and said, "Well, did you come to any conclusion?"

His father looked at the end of his cigar, which had gone out. He reached in his pocket for a box of matches. "Ellie tells me you're grown-up. I guess if you're grown-up, you're able to make your own decisions about your life." He paused and struck a match, but it went out. "Just before you go in for your physical, press your hand against your temple..." He showed him the place. "Keep up the pressure for a few minutes. I think it'll slow you down." As Jed's face lit up, the doctor said, "Mind you, I don't guarantee it. You'll just have to hope it works."

"Yeeow!" Jed slapped his father's shoulder and then grabbed Elinor and swung her off her feet. " 'Off we go, into the wild blue yonder . . .' "

Cy, beaming, made a wild swoop with his arm to indicate a plane.

"Your mother's going to have my hide for this," Dr. Winslow said. "Let's take a long walk down the beach so I can enjoy the day before I get lambasted."

"We'll defend you, Dad," Cy said. "Us guys will man the barricades." He ran in a wide circle around them, flailing his arms.

"Cut it out, Cy," the doctor said sharply. "It's not a game we're talking about."

Cy quieted down quickly. "Sorry."

When they reached the cove, they stopped. While Cy showed his father a dead jellyfish behind some of the eight-foot-tall granite rocks, Jed took advantage of the moment of privacy. He put his arms around Elinor and kissed her.

"You brought it off for me." His eyes were shining.

He had never kissed her like that before. She felt almost too stunned to answer. All she could think of was that she hoped she hadn't doomed him. "I'm getting so I can write a little better," she said, trying to hold onto her self-possession. "I'll write to you."

When they got back to the house, a call was waiting for the doctor.

"The Andrews boy tripped over his bicycle, and his mother thinks his arm is broken," Mrs. Winslow said. "It's all out of shape, she says. I told her not to move him till you get there."

The doctor had picked up his bag and was already going out the door. "Fell over his bicycle," he said, shaking his head. "Fell over his own big feet. Nice you could come, Claire, and you, Ellie." And he was hurrying to his car.

Mrs. Winslow looked at Jed's face and said bleakly, "He told you, didn't he. You'll pass the test now."

"Mom . . ." Jed looked at her, pained at her pain. "It may not work."

"It will work." She turned away.

"Elinor, we must go. It's been such a lovely day, I can hardly tear myself away." Elinor's mother got up, and Cy got her coat. "Thank you, Cy. Emma, it was so sweet of you to think of us . . ." For a moment she choked up, but she covered it by giving Mrs. Winslow a quick embrace. Recovering her smile, she said, "You must come over soon. We see each other all too seldom these days."

Mrs. Winslow and Jed walked with the Goldens to their car. "It made a lovely day for us, having you. Thank you for coming."

"I'll drive, Mother," Elinor said.

"All right. I hate to drive."

Mrs. Winslow said to Elinor, "Come often. We have much to talk about." Her eyes were warm and affectionate, and Elinor felt like a traitor. But perhaps what she had said to Dr. Winslow hadn't really been the thing that had made up his mind. Adults didn't usually turn to kids for major decisions. He must have known he was going to give in. But she suffered for Jed's mother. And for herself.

"It was a nice day, wasn't it?" she said to her mother as they drove away.

"Lovely." Her mother sounded far away. "It was good of them to ask us. I suppose they felt sorry for us."

"Oh, I don't think it was that."

"I despise pity," her mother said with sudden vehemence. "To be an object of pity is the most shameful thing that can happen to one."

Elinor felt discouraged. She had really thought her mother had gotten her mind off things for a little while. "Nothing is shameful, is it, that isn't your own fault," she said, knowing it was futile to argue.

"Many people, I'm sure, see it as my fault. A wife who can't hold her husband . . . there must be something wrong with her. That's what people think."

Elinor knew she should just keep still but she couldn't resist saying, "Maybe people aren't thinking about it as much as you think. Everybody's got so many problems of their own now. . . ."

Her mother turned her face to the window, and Elinor couldn't tell whether she was weeping or not. Wasn't this ever going to end? And yet she felt cruel thinking that. When somebody suffered, they couldn't turn it off like a faucet after a prescribed period of time. She drove faster than she meant to, and skidded as she turned into their street.

"Do be careful," her mother said.

The snow had stopped, but it was cold. When they got to the garage, Elinor sat for a minute, still holding the wheel. For some reason she dreaded going into the empty house.

"Aren't you coming?" her mother said as she got out.

"Sure. Just a sec. I'll lock up the garage." When her mother had gone in, Elinor locked up, trying not to look at the garage space where her father's car used to be parked. Things that belonged to him were all over the garage. Tools, old sneakers, a stack of medical magazines that hadn't gotten out to the trash can. I'm as bad as Mother, she thought, moping around. She snapped the lock on the garage door.

The wind had scrubbed the sky until the stars shone.

She sat down for a minute in the old swing that hung from the oak tree. The rope creaked. For the first time it occurred to her that her mother might remarry some day. She was still attractive, and men liked her. That would be the best solution, only it seemed awfully strange. You expect your parents to stay fixed, like the stars. She stared up at the stars through the bare branches of the tree. Only stars really didn't stay fixed. They were always exploding and zooming off into space and colliding. Nothing was really fixed. That upset her.

She tipped her head on one side, hearing the barely audible sound of an airplane. Automatically she looked for its lights and found them, moving like colored dots among the stars. Her mind recited the formula: single engine plane, lights visible, high, out of the northeast heading west. . . . And someday soon Jed's plane would be up there, hurtling through the sky, like a star gone wild.

"Elinor, what are you doing?" Her mother called from the kitchen door.

"Coming." She got up and walked slowly toward the house. The ropes of the swing creaked as it went on swinging for a moment and gradually slowed to a stop, the seat a little crooked because nobody had adjusted the ropes for a long time.

CHAPTER SIXTEEN

Elinor couldn't believe what she heard on the radio on December 7. The Japanese had bombed Pearl Harbor. At first she didn't know where Pearl Harbor was, and the excitment of the radio announcers made the news hard to follow. She called to her mother.

"The Japanese have bombed us."

Her mother, still in the clothes she had worn to church, came into Elinor's room. "Bombed what?"

Together they listened as the reports came in. Eight battleships sunk, three cruisers, one hundred eighty-eight planes. Twenty-four hundred men, American men, killed.

"It couldn't be another one of those Orson Welles things, could it?"

Elinor shook her head. "I guess it's real, all right."

After a few minutes her mother said, "Well, I've got to get the roast in, war or no war." She went downstairs.

For the rest of the day and late into the night Elinor kept her radio on. Her father called her, sounding excited and upset. He kept saying, "Twenty-four hundred men killed. They never had a chance."

Early the next day Elinor woke and turned on the radio again. She heard the statement of the President: "Yesterday, December 7, 1941, a date which will live in infamy." Then came the announcements that Japan had declared war on the United States and Great Britain, and they in turn had declared war on Japan. "Declared war" seemed a meaningless act, in the light of what had happened.

She tried to get used to thinking of Japan as an enemy. People had talked about Japan, and there had been things in the paper. Shortly after the president signed the Selective Service Act more than a year ago, Japan had officially joined Germany and Italy in the Axis. And last July the United States had frozen Japanese assets in America. But somehow she hadn't paid much attention. To her the enemy was Germany, or had been. Now everything was different. In some ways actually being at war was almost a relief, because the threat of it no longer hung overhead. Five months ago, when President Roosevelt had proclaimed an unlimited national emergency, it had felt like war and yet hadn't really been so. Now things were not so much radically changed as simply more so.

Later in the week when her mother suggested a Christmas party for Tom, Elinor was a little shocked. It seemed frivolous to talk about parties. But on the other hand Tom was in the service, and he should have all the cheering up they could give him. He had only a four day pass, so they had a narrow choice of dates. Elinor's mother couldn't resist doing some of the planning, but she left most of the guest list and many of the details to Elinor.

"It must be a perfect party," she said, with more interest than she had shown in anything for a long time. "No sadness, no worries, just a wonderful party that he'll always remember."

Elinor was touched, and she did her best to cooperate. There were a few minor arguments over the guest list until her mother abruptly gave in and said, "All right, do it your way, but check the final list with Tom as soon as he gets home, in case we've left anyone out."

"I'll mail him a list. We can't wait that late to invite anyone."

"All right. I'll write out the list for you."

"I can do it." Elinor had been going to Jed's house twice a week, at Dr. Winslow's suggestion, and practicing word exercises, both reading and writing, with Mrs. Winslow. She had made some slow improvement. At home she also practiced at night on an old typewriter of her father's. She wanted to show off her new ability to her brother. "You can check it before I send it," she said to her mother.

She worked very carefully on the list, remembering who Tom's favorite friends were, who would be in town, who got along with whom. Theoretically it was her party, too, so she included about a dozen of her own friends.

Jed, of course. He had passed his physical for the Air Corps and he would be leaving for Lowry Field in Denver right after the first of the year.

She called Ben's sister to see if Ben would be home but the sister said no. Elinor invited her to the party, because she was a classmate of Tom's. She sounded pleased. Their mother had died, and she was staying at home to keep house for her father. She seemed so lonely, Elinor was glad she'd thought of asking her. Elinor could see herself in Betty's role, stuck at home to look after a parent, friends leaving to live their own lives, boys going away and marrying other girls. But she was not going to let it happen to her.

When she had the list finished, there were thirty names in addition to Tom and herself. While she was waiting for Tom to answer about the names she had laboriously typed out, she bought invitations and began to address them using a ruler. She was determined to do this herself, but it took her a long time, and at least a dozen of the little invitation cards were thrown away before she got to the end of the list. She showed them to her mother to make sure they were all right, no reversed letters or anything. There were four mistakes.

"They're very neatly printed," her mother said, looking at her. She was quite illogical about Elinor's trouble with words. She refused to admit that there was a real problem, yet she obviously didn't think Elinor could write or read normally. She seemed irritated when Elinor went to the Winslows' to practice the tracing and memorizing of words. "It's a notion of your father's," she had said. "It's absurd. He blows everything up so." But she had not forbidden her to go.

And she invited Dr. and Mrs. Winslow to have Tom-and-Jerries with her in the upstairs library on the night of the party. "I'll need your moral support, Emma," she said to Mrs. Winslow on the phone. "Thirty-two young people in my house! I don't think I could handle it."

Tom came home the day before, enthusiastic about the party and about being home, and full of tales about officers' training. He had a few routine complaints, but on the whole it was clear that he enjoyed it.

"Wait till they get you in their clutches, boy," he said to Jed. "It's an eye-popping experience."

The two spent a lot of time talking, the age gap between them forgotten. Listening to them, Elinor felt like a stranger. Men involved in the war had some kind of bond that no one else could penetrate. She thought it was sad that it took a war to bring them together in that mood of fellowship. Tom had never paid much attention to Jed before, except in the casual kidding way that he treated all of Elinor's friends. But he was impressed by Jed's new status as an Air Corps cadet.

When Elinor had learned that Miss Jones was not going home for Christmas, she had impulsively asked her to the party without consulting her mother or Tom. Miss Jones had accepted. After all, Elinor thought, as she prepared to justify herself to her mother, Miss Jones had been nice to her. And she wasn't more than a couple of years older than Tom and his friends. Her mother had frowned when she told her, but made no objection.

The day of the party, friends home from college dropped by to see her and to offer help. It was good to see them, but their tales of college made her feel lonely. Even Julie seemed different, older, more experienced.

On December twenty-third, the night of the party, a soft Christmas snow began to fall early in the evening. The wreath on the front door was dusted with snow by the time the first guests arrived. In the living room, rugs were rolled back for dancing, candles flickered on the mantel, records were neatly stacked beside the record player, and a Tommy Dorsey record was playing "Sentimental Journey." The big Christmas tree in the corner was lighted. The table in the dining room had a poinsettia plant in the center, surrounded by tiny angels that Elinor had discovered in a shop downtown. On one end of the table a punchbowl gleamed, and at the other end was a bowl of eggnog, piled high with the beaten egg whites that Tom had added at the last moment. There were bowls of freshly popped corn, plates of sandwiches "big enough for people to get their teeth into," Tom had said, arguing against his mother's notion of tiny sandwiches with the crusts off. There was a bowl of cold shrimp in a remoulade sauce, and a platter of sliced baked ham, cold roast chicken, and smoked turkey. Celery, radishes, pickles. And S.S. Pierce fruit cake, sliced thin.

In out of the way corners some card tables were set up, with new decks of cards and scorepads on them, for any who wanted to play bridge.

Elinor beamed at the exclamations of pleasure from the guests. Julie helped her take the coats upstairs to the bedrooms. Tom greeted the guests, shook hands, laughed, joked.

There were some uniforms among the guests. Tom's friend Ollie Cox was in the Coast Guard. Elinor's classmate Joe Lasky, home from basic training in the Field Artillery at Camp Edwards, was proud of his newly acquired private first class stripe. And another of Tom's friends, Bradley Fullerton, was a Navy ensign.

"Big deal," he told Tom. "I've got a desk job in Charlestown. Looks like I'll never get any further than the Bunker Hill Monument."

"Cheer up, son," Tom said. "With your picturesque phiz, they'll probably make you admiral of the fleet, just so they can get a good picture in the papers. Hey, Ellie, will you get the admiral's coat? Hi, Dick, boy, glad to see you. How's everything at Princeton?"

Elinor waited to take Dick Prentiss's coat upstairs, as well as Brad's. She had always had a secret crush on Dick Prentiss, who looked, she thought, like Scott Fitzgerald and was very superior. Brad was better-looking, but Dick represented a sophisticated college world that seemed more interesting than Harvard or Dartmouth, perhaps because it was farther away.

"Can you manage?" Dick gave her one of his rare smiles as she put his coat on top of Brad's.

He laughed when she said, "Oh, sure," and then staggered slightly as she started for the stairs. "Here, I'll give you a hand," he said. He took both coats. "Tell me which room."

"The big bedroom at the top of the stairs, but really, I could take them . . ." She stopped because he was already halfway up the stairs. She had felt the whack of something hard in his coat pocket, and she suspected it was a flask. If he took a nip up in the bedroom, she hoped her mother wouldn't walk in on him. Her mother knew perfectly well that young people, including Tom, drank at parties, but she liked to pretend that she disapproved. Tom was waiting till she was upstairs for the evening before he brought out the second bowl of punch, spiked with gin. And there would be quiet little trips to the kitchen where the half-gallon of Tanqueray was stashed away in the pantry.

"I don't really care if she discovers it," Tom had said to Elinor. "After all, I'm not a child. But she feels it's her duty to make a fuss, and why put her through that?"

While Elinor greeted two more of her friends, her mother came down the stairs, looking pretty in a long chiffon dinner gown. She circulated through the rooms, speaking to the guests. When she had completed the rounds, she went back upstairs to rejoin Dr. and Mrs. Winslow in her own small sitting room. Elinor knew she would not be down again.

Miss Jones came, just as Elinor had begun to think she was not coming. She saw the appreciative light in Tom's eyes when she introduced them.

"I've heard so much about you," he said. "Here, let me have your coat."

"Thank you," Miss Jones said. "Elinor, your house looks so attractive."

Elinor blushed. She felt shy with Miss Jones in this setting. But there was no need for her to do anything; Tom was giving the teacher his full attention. Elinor turned away as Jed came up.

"Let's dance," Jed said.

"I have to cart the coats upstairs."

"Almost everybody must be here by now. Let Tom carry them. Come on, let's dance."

A few couples were already dancing to a Jimmy Dorsey record. Others stood around the record player. They were arguing about who the best jazz instrumentalists were.

"Artie Shaw," somebody said.

"No, no, Goodman is a million times better."

"Jack Teagarden," Joe Lasky said. "Who do you say, Ellie?"

"Gosh, I don't know. There are so many good ones. I like Roy Bargy awfully well. And Teddy Wilson ..."

"Bix Beiderbecke is the best by every standard there is," Jed said.

"But he's dead. We're talking about now."

"All right. Billy Butterfield." Jed swung Elinor around, and they began to jitterbug.

At that moment everything began to come together for Elinor, the excitement of the party, the pleasure of being with her friends again, the poignancy of the departures soon to come for the boys in the service, the insistent beat of the music, Jed. She let herself go with more than usual abandonment to the music. Jed caught her mood. They had never danced better.

When the record stopped there was applause. Surprised and a little flustered, she saw that the others had stopped dancing to watch Jed and her.

"Boy, that was swell!" Joe said.

"They can really dance, can't they?" Julie said to Alice Blaine.

"They've been dancing together since they were practically babies," Alice said.

Dick Prentiss, who had joined the group, smiled his sardonic little Princeton smile, and said, "Ellie, they don't dance any better than that in Princeton."

"Naturally not," said Joe. "They're all guys."

Dick made a wry face. "We do have girls around at times, Lasky."

Jed took Elinor's hand and they went into the dining room for some punch.

"That one has gin in it," Elinor said, pointing to the second punch bowl.

"Good." Jed grinned and poured himself a cup. "Us Air Corps guys are heavy drinkers."

Elinor could see Tom dancing with Miss Jones. She hoped he didn't get too carried away. He was the host —he was supposed to dance with everybody, or at least talk to them.

She left Jed with the punch and a cucumber sandwich, when Joe came and asked her to dance. Joe wasn't as good as Jed, but he was good, and Elinor liked him. He was a little guy, quick with jokes, never a big success with the girls because he was short, and never good at team sports. When they were in high school together, she had always thought of him as an outsider, like herself. People liked him, but they forgot to ask him to parties, overlooked him in school activities, except on the debating team, where his wit made him a good debater. She and Joe had always been friends.

The party was going well, she thought. The two age groups stayed apart, mostly, Tom's friends dancing or playing bridge or talking with each other, while Elinor's friends tended to huddle in groups to listen to the music or to fill their punch cups in the dining room and to talk. But Tom danced with the younger girls too, and most of his friends danced with her, even Dick Prentiss, although she was so nervous with him, she couldn't think of anything intelligent to say, and once she stepped on his foot.

Tom saw to it that Miss Jones met the other guests,

and soon she was involved in a concentrated bridge game with Ollie Cox, Brad Fullerton, and Brad's girl, Jenny Weston. She seemed to be enjoying herself.

Alice Blaine said, "Ellie, I knew the invitation was from you even before I read it. Know how?"

"No," Elinor said. She didn't want to hear. Alice was not the world's most tactful girl. I must have done something wrong, Elinor thought.

Alice looked around at the others. "I knew it was old Ellie right away, when I looked in the corner and it said 'R.S.P.V.'" She laughed with delight. She was not exactly malicious, but she had always delighted in other people's discomfiture.

The others looked embarrassed, and Joe said, "Oh, shut your big mouth, Al."

Jed, who had just joined the group, said, "That's a sign of genius, you know, reversing letters. You know what a genius is, don't you, Alice?" Before she could answer, he took Elinor's arm and steered her away to another part of the room. "Hey, have you been around your father's office? I mean the one that used to be his office." He pointed to Mrs. Golden's sewing room.

"Not lately," Elinor said. She felt uncomfortable, as if Alice had bumped into a painful bruise. "Why?"

"Marcie brought a package of those crazy cigarettes that she smokes—you know, the colored ones with gold tips, that are perfumed. The room smells like an opium den or something."

They went across the hall to the room and looked in. Marcie and four others were puffing away vigorously on the pastel-tinted cigarettes.

"Come on in," Marcie said. "Join us."

Jed was laughing. "Mrs. Golden will have to fumigate this room before she can use it. Wait till she gets a load of that smoke!"

Marcie sat down on Harold Dean's lap. "Come on in and be decadent with us." These were Tom's friends, but Elinor knew Marcie well because Tom had gone with her for several years.

She smiled. "Thanks, Marcie, but I've got to circulate. Have fun."

As they walked away, Jed said, "I take it Ben Barker was not home on leave."

Elinor put her hand to her mouth. "Betty!" She looked around the crowded room. "Betty Barker isn't here, is she?"

"Haven't seen her."

"Ben didn't get home, but I invited Betty and she said she'd come."

"Maybe her old man wouldn't let her have the car. He's such a slob. Why don't you call her up? If she needs transportation, I can go get her."

Elinor and Jed went into the kitchen to use the phone there. Elinor found Betty's phone number and gave it to the operator. She could hear the Barkers' phone ringing, but there was no answer. She was about to hang up when Betty's voice said, "Hello?" She sounded strange.

"Betty?"

"Yes?"

"This is Elinor." When there was no answer, she said, "Elinor Golden."

"Oh," Betty said. "Yes."

Elinor was disconcerted. "I thought maybe . . . uh . . . I was hoping you were coming to my party." Still no reply. "If you need transportation, Jed will come get you."

Finally Betty said, "I can't come." .

"Oh. I'm sorry. Maybe some other time. Merry Christmas anyway. When you write to Ben, tell him hi for me." She was about to hang up when Betty spoke.

"Ben's gone."

"What? What, Betty?"

"Ben."

"What do you mean? Gone to sea?"

"Lost," Betty said. " 'Missing, presumed dead.' In the Atlantic."

"Betty!"

"The telegram came from the Navy this afternoon."

"Oh, Betty!" She heard Betty burst into tears and hang up. For a minute she held the telephone in her hands, the receiver against her ear, as if there must be more to hear. Then slowly she put the receiver back on the cradle and turned to Jed.

"What is it?" he said. "Can't she come? What's the matter?"

Elinor felt stunned, and yet it was something she had felt all along was going to happen. "It's Ben."

"What about Ben?"

"He's lost. Missing, presumed dead . . . . dead."

"My God!" Jed said softly. He took her hand. "Did Betty tell you?"

"Yes. The Navy sent them a telegram. She was crying."

"What kind of ship was he on?"

"He couldn't tell me, but I had an idea, I don't know why, that he was on a submarine in the Atlantic."

"Yeah. They've been escorting Lend-Lease ships. Some U-boat must have got them." He put his arm around her. "I'm so sorry."

"He was so proud of being in the Navy."

Jed stepped away from her at the sound of voices.

"Don't let's tell them now," she said.

"All right."

Tom and Miss Jones came into the kitchen.

"Hi," Tom said. "What are you two up to, or should I ask?" He got the bottle of gin and looked at it. "Getting low."

"Just ginger ale for me," Miss Jones said.

"Are you sure?" Tom said. "I have Scotch if you prefer . . ."

"No, really. The School Board frowns on booze." She smiled at Elinor. "It's a lovely party. I'm so glad you asked me."

Elinor's face felt stiff when she tried to smile. "I'm glad you're having a good time." She took Jed's hand, and they left the kitchen. "I wish the party were over," she told him.

"Listen, I'll be hanging around whenever you need moral support. Just give me the high sign."

She nodded and squeezed his hand, hating to leave him but remembering she was the hostess. She checked on the food supply in the dining room, and urged everyone to come and eat. Soon most people were crowding into the dining room, filling plates and telling her how good the food was. She got Jed to refill the punch bowl.

Dick Prentiss filled four plates and balanced them precariously along his arm, heading for one of the bridge tables. Elinor was glad her mother couldn't see her best china so dangerously poised. But she didn't hear any crash, so he must have made it.

She ladled out eggnog for a while, and Jed took charge of the punch bowl. Tom brought in a big silver coffee pot with freshly brewed coffee.

134

Elinor felt as if she were walking through a difficult dream that seemed as if it would never end. She heard herself talking, saying the more or less right thing at the right time, doing what she was supposed to do. But every so often she had an almost irresistible urge to run out of the house into the dark, snowy night. When that feeling hit, she looked for Jed and he was always right there in a second, talking to her quietly about nothing important, touching her hand, just being there. She tried hardest of all to keep out of her mind the thought that it could some day be a telegram about Jed or Tom. That didn't bear thinking of, and yet the idea hovered around her mind like a huge bird threatening to attack.

Eventually the party came to an end. The last guest, except Jed, had gone. Tom had taken Miss Jones home because she had come in a taxi; her car had frozen up. Dr. and Mrs. Winslow and Elinor's mother came downstairs after the cars had driven off and the last calls of "Merry Christmas" had died away.

Mrs. Golden surveyed the remains of the party and sighed. "My word, what chaos."

"I'll clean it up," Elinor said quickly. "It'll be all back to normal by morning, Mother."

"It sounded like a gay party," Mrs. Winslow said. "Did you have fun?"

"It was a fine party." Jed looked at Elinor, who nodded. "Only there was some bad news." He took a breath. "Ben Barker has been killed at sea."

"Missing, presumed dead," Elinor said quickly. It didn't sound quite as stark as "killed." But of course it was. A person shouldn't try to kid herself.

Dr. Winslow said, "Oh, no," and walked quickly to the window and stared out.

"Oh, dear," Mrs. Winslow said. "Oh, his poor father."

"Barker?" Elinor's mother said. "That's the boy you went to the movies with, isn't it?"

"Yes."

"How did it happen?"

Elinor wasn't sure she should mention the submarine. If it had been secret before, it would still be secret. She said, "I don't know. The Barkers don't have any details yet, I guess." She saw the little look of approval Jed gave her. She was right not to mention the submarine. After all, it was only her guess. There was a lot in the papers about the danger of spreading rumors.

"That news must have thrown a damper on the party," Mrs. Golden said.

"Ellie didn't tell them," Jed said. He put his hand on Elinor's shoulder for a second. "She was great. She carried on as if nothing had happened."

Dr. Winslow came back to the group. "Good girl," he said quietly. His eyes were red. "I brought those Barker kids into the world. I liked Ben. Nice boy." He clamped his jaws together and took his wife's arm. "Got to be going. Nice evening, Claire. Enjoyed it."

"And you didn't get called away once," Elinor's mother said. She got their coats from the hall closet. "I'm so glad you came. I wouldn't have known what to do with myself." To Elinor she said. "Where's Tom?"

"He took Miss Jones home. Her car froze up."

"Oh. He brought her upstairs to meet us."

"She seems like a bright young woman," Dr. Winslow said. He thrust his arms into his heavy coat and wrapped a long woolen muffler around his neck. "Never had pretty teachers like that in my day. All old maiden ladies, that's what we had."

"Those 'old maiden ladies' were often wonderful teachers," his wife said.

"Yes, you're right, you're right. But I never had any romantic dreams about them."

"It's just as well." Mrs. Winslow kissed Mrs. Golden on the cheek. "Have a good Christmas, my dear. We have our children."

Elinor's mother choked up. "Who knows how soon again . . ."

"Now, now, now, Claire," Dr. Winslow said. "Enjoy the present while it's here. The future will take care of itself." He hugged her and then he hugged Elinor. "Merry Christmas, my dear."

"Are you coming with us, son?" Mrs. Winslow said.

"No, I'm going to help Ellie clean up."

"Oh, Jed, you don't need to do that," Elinor's mother said. "Tom and Elinor can do it . . ."

"I'd like to," he said firmly.

When the Winslows had gone, Jed and Elinor began to take the dirty dishes to the kitchen. For some time they didn't talk, except about what they were doing. Then Elinor put down a trayful of glasses and began to cry quietly. Jed put his arms around her, her head on his shoulder.

"Go ahead and cry, honey," he said. "It's better to cry." He held her for several minutes. When she took a deep breath and straightened up, he gave her his handkerchief. She wiped her eyes.

"Don't boys ever cry?" she said.

"Sure. I didn't know Ben well enough to cry for him, I guess. Although to tell you the truth, sometimes I feel like crying for all the people, all the perfectly nice, decent people that I don't even know, who are dying because of some maniacs in Berlin and Tokyo. Then I get mad."

The lights from her mother's car, which Tom had used to take Miss Jones home, lit up the driveway.

"I'll tell Tom," she said. "But I won't cry any more."

"Gosh, I'm going to miss you," he said.

"Are you?" She smiled. "That's nice. But don't think about it now. Remember what your dad said. One day at a time, or whatever it was. And now I can write to you, anyway after a fashion." And as Tom burst into the kitchen, red-cheeked and smiling, she braced herself to tell him about Ben Barker.

CHAPTER SEVENTEEN

Tom and Elinor stood out at the end of the driveway waiting for their father to pick them up. They were going to spend Christmas Eve with him.

"It's crazy, isn't it, hanging around here for our own father," Tom said.

"Yes. But Mother goes into such a fit if she thinks he's coming near the house."

"I can't get used to it."

"I know." She waved. "Here he comes."

They crossed the street and got into their father's car. Elinor looked back at the house and saw the curtain move.

Her mother had been watching. It was so pathetic, it could break your heart, she thought. For a minute she felt angry with her father for apparently being so well-adjusted to the new state of things. But when she looked at him, she realized he was tired.

"You look bushed," she said.

He nodded. "We lost a patient this morning. It gives you a bad feeling."

"Anyone we know?" Tom asked.

"A fellow from Rhode Island. Up here to visit relatives for Christmas. They brought him in with a belly-ache. He died of peritonitis."

"Was he young?"

Dr. Golden shrugged. "Forty. Too young to die."

"You heard about Ben Barker, I suppose."

"Yes. Rotten shame. Poor Betty."

"Well, I guess we should cheer up a little," Tom said. "It's Christmas Eve. Want me to drive, Dad, if you're tired?"

"Yeah, why don't you." He stopped the car, and they changed places.

Tom drove out the cross-country roads to the New-buryport turnpike. It was cold and cloudy, and by five o'clock it was dark. Elinor glanced at her father, who sat with his head back and his eyes closed. They rode in silence for some time. The northbound traffic was fairly heavy, but there was almost no one heading toward Boston.

The doctor opened his eyes and said, "Pull into the Fo'c'sle," he said. "I need a drink."

Tom drove off the turnpike into the parking lot of the big restaurant and bar that was shaped like a ship. Except for three people having an early meal, there was no one there except the staff.

They sat at the bar. The bartender gave the bar a quick wipe with a damp cloth. "How are you, Doc?"

"Lousy, Harry. Merry Christmas."

"The usual?"

"Right. These are my youngsters."

"Pleased to meet you," Harry said. "What'll you have?" He was a pleasant-faced man, middle-aged, with a single strand of hair carefully combed over the top of his bald head.

"Scotch and soda," Tom said.

Elinor hesitated. "Sherry, please." She hadn't done much drinking, and she had never sat up at a bar before.

"Dry, sweet, medium?"

"Dry." That sounded more sophisticated than "sweet." She had no idea whether the sherry she had had before had been dry or what. She felt grown-up sitting there with her father and her brother, being taken for granted as if she always did this.

"Not much business tonight, Harry," her father said.

"Nope. Everybody's home wrapping presents." He expertly mixed the doctor's martini, and slid Tom's Scotch along the counter so that it stopped exactly in front of Tom. He poured Elinor's sherry in a long-stemmed glass. "There you are, young lady." He settled back against the cash register with his arms folded, and looked at Tom's uniform. "What outfit you in, son?" He was interested when Tom told him. "Didn't know we had soldiers on skiis. Good idea, I guess. We gotta get at them bastards somehow. . . . Excuse me, young lady, excuse my French."

"That's all right."

141

"Funny thing, ain't it," he said, "the way people can think up all kinds of nice things, like Christmas trees and the like of that, and doctors workin' so hard to make people well, and yet you let some son-of-a . . . some son-of-a-gun come along and get a war started, and it all goes down the drain."

"Yes," Dr. Golden said gloomily. "It makes you wonder. Are we always going to cancel out the good with the evil? I don't know. Man is a funny critter."

"Well, that's life, I guess." Harry turned on the radio, and they sat quietly drinking their drinks and listening to Christmas carols.

The doctor put his empty glass down. "Merry Christmas to you, Harry, if that's possible these days." He slipped a dollar tip under the glass.

"Thanks a lot, Doc. That's real nice. See you after Christmas. Merry Christmas, all of you. Keep 'em flyin'."

When they were on their way again, Tom said, "Do you stop in every night?"

"Usually. It gives me a lift to make it the rest of the way home."

Elinor was thinking about Harry. "He was nice."

"Yeah, he's a good guy."

She liked listening to the things men said to each other in a place like that. Sometimes she and Jed ended up their evenings at the diner, lingering over a hamburger and a cup of coffee, listening to the men who seemed to sit there eternally. They said things like "Sit down and take a load off," and "Don't take no wooden nickels," and "See you in church," meaningless phrases so worn that they felt comfortable. It was like a ritual that they all knew.

142

"I forgot to ask you how your party went," her father said. He seemed to have perked up some after the drink.

"Fine," Tom said. "It was a great party."

"Except that we found out about Ben," Elinor said.

"Ellie knew it in the middle of the party but she never let on, so nobody's night was spoiled." Tom paused. "I met Ellie's teacher, the Jones girl. She came. She's a real dish."

"Don't say things like that," Elinor said. "I hate it when boys say things like that."

"Sorry. I mean she was very attractive. I saw her home. And this morning I got a twenty-minute lecture from Mother on the inadvisability of courting older women." He laughed, but he sounded irritated. "All I did, you understand, was talk to the girl a little while, dance with her twice, and see her home because her car was frozen. This is courting?"

"Your mother is sensitive on that subject because she's two years older than I am," his father said. "I never could see what difference it made."

"Mother can really build a mountain out of ye olde molehill."

"Well, she upsets herself more than anybody else," Elinor said. She wished Tom wouldn't talk about it.

"She's her own worst enemy," Tom said. "She drives away the people she cares about because she can't let them be free. I mean a guy can't breathe . . ."

"Oh, shut up, Tommy," Elinor said. "You're free enough."

"Yes," her father said, "let's don't psychoanalyze your mother."

Tom muttered something under his breath and didn't

talk again until they came into Charles Street. Elinor had heard him arguing with their mother that morning, but she hadn't realized he was so upset about it. She wished she could make her mother see how she alienated people. It was a shame.

"Where are we going for dinner?" Tom asked.

"I thought maybe the Old Oyster House. I made a reservation for seven-thirty."

"Oh, good," Elinor said. "I love that place."

"Is Elsa going with us?"

"No, she may drop by later in the evening for a drink."

In the apartment he had decorated a small tree and there were wrapped presents under it. Elinor felt touched and sad, for some reason. She hoped he would like the scarf she had knitted for him. Because she had trouble with the directions, she wasn't the world's best knitter, as her mother was fond of telling her, but she had worked hard on this scarf. She'd unraveled and reknit half a dozen times. It was, she thought, very pretty wool, dark green.

As soon as her father had showered and changed his clothes and made a pitcher of martinis, they sat down to open their presents. He offered her another glass of sherry, but she decided she'd had enough for now. At home her mother had nagged a lot about the nightly martinis, and she realized it must be a relief for him to be able to have a couple of drinks without having to justify it. But there was enough of her mother's training in her to make her hope he wasn't overdoing it. I'd probably be a nag and a worrier just like Mother, she thought, if I were somebody's wife.

She opened one of the presents he had given her and squealed with delight. It was a beautiful, soft blue cashmere sweater from Jay's. He looked pleased at her enthusiasm.

For Tom there was a waterproof wristwatch with thin bands of steel over the crystal to keep it from breaking. Tom was pleased.

"Look, it's got a sweep second hand." He showed it to Elinor.

"It'll take a lot of guff, the man said," his father told him. "Shockproof and all that, whatever that's good for."

Elinor put the wrapped scarf in his lap. "I hope it'll be all right . . ."

He gave her his radiant smile. "Of course it will, honey." He opened the package and held up the scarf. It did look pretty, and in the soft light you couldn't see where she'd wandered a bit from the pattern. "It's great, Ellie. Just what I need." He got up and kissed her and wrapped the scarf around his neck. "It'll keep me warm on that darned turnpike."

Tom gave him a fifth of Jamieson Irish whiskey.

His father laughed. "You've got your old man pegged. That's really nice, Tom. After dinner I'll whip us up some Irish coffee."

Then there were the other presents from him—a sterling pen and pencil set for Tom, and a leather toilet case from Mark Cross. For Elinor there was a gaily-colored stocking cap with a long tassel, and a bottle of Chanel. Each of them got a check for twenty-five dollars.

Elinor put on the stocking cap. "This will be wonderful when I go plane spotting."

"That's what I had in mind." He seemed much more cheerful now. He looked at his watch. "We'd better get crackin.' It's almost time for our reservation."

Elinor hadn't been to the Old Oyster House for ages.

She loved its creaky old booths and the sawdust-covered floor. When they returned to the apartment, they walked slowly up the hill, looking at the pretty Christmas lights. It was hard to think of war, except that there were so many young men in uniform wandering around. Hundreds of sailors on the Common and along Tremont Street. The Charlestown Navy Yard was not far away.

While their father was preparing the Irish coffees, Elsa came. She looked very attractive in her fur coat and close-fitting fur hat. Her cheeks were red from the cold.

She seemed friendlier than she had the last time, less bitter and critical. She talked about a job she had found, working as a secretary at the Women's Educational and Industrial Union. She seemed resigned to it, but Elinor's father shook his head.

"Can you beat that? It's like the Old Corner Bookstore hiring Einstein as a stockroom boy."

That struck Elinor as rather an extreme comparison, and even Elsa laughed at him but she seemed pleased.

"*C'est la guerre, mon ami.* We all do odd things in the war. Look at your boy—he belongs in law school, does he not? But he is in uniform."

Tom raised his cup of Irish coffee. "Here's to peace and dignity and decency."

His toast made Elinor feel shivery. So much of the time he kidded, but when he was serious, he was very serious. They all raised their cups in silence and drank to his toast. The Irish coffee was wonderful. It didn't taste much like whiskey at all, perhaps because her father hadn't put much in her cup. She loved drinking the hot coffee through the topping of whipped cream. Her father knew how to do things.

"Listen," he said. "The bellringers."

They went out and stood on the brick steps, listening to the caroling bellringers working their way up the hill. Her father stood a step above Elsa, his hand lightly on her shoulder in a posture somehow more intimate than an embrace. She felt the same stab of jealousy that she had had before. She didn't want him to be so close to this alien woman.

As the bellringers played "Silent Night," he sang it softly in German. ". . . heilige nacht . . ."

Elsa turned her head to look up at him. There were tears in her eyes.

When the carolers had gone, they went inside and Tom helped his father take the coffee things into the little kitchen. Elsa and Elinor were left alone for a few minutes.

Because of the unexpected softness and loneliness she had seen in Elsa's face, Elinor made an effort to be nice. "When I was little, my mother used to take me to the bookshop at the Women's Educational and Industrial Union," she said. "It was nice."

"Do you not go to bookshops now?" The softness was gone. She had the sharp, critical tone she had had on their first meeting. Elinor wondered if the mention of her mother had been tactless.

"Not much. I have a reading problem."

"Oh, yes. Your father told me." She studied Elinor for a long, disconcerting moment. "Why then are you in school?"

Elinor tried to laugh it off. "I'm not sure, really."

"Why don't you get a job?"

"A job?"

"Yes, a job. Work. In Europe at your age women are either in the university or at work."

Elinor began to feel angry. It wasn't her fault that she was stuck in the school. She would much rather work. "I'm not allowed to," she said, and instantly regretted it. It sounded childish, and she saw Elsa's flash of contempt.

"Allowed to! You are . . . how old? Eighteen?"

"Yes." Elinor wished her father would come back. She was afraid she would lose her temper and tell this woman off. What business was it of hers what Elinor did?

"In England at eighteen the girls are already serving with the Army, the Air Force, the Red Cross . . ."

"And in Germany also?" It was an unforgivable thing to say, and she was ashamed of herself.

Elsa stood up so suddenly, Elinor thought for a second that she was going to hit her. But she only walked away, looked out the window, and said, "In Germany also."

At that moment Tom and his father returned. The doctor looked quickly from Elinor to Elsa and back, sensing the tension.

"We'd better go," Tom said, "or we'll miss the last train."

"Elsa, come with me while I take the children to North Station," the doctor said.

"No," she said, "I must go."

"We can take a cab," Tom said.

"Of course not." His father sounded gruff. "Get your things together. Can I drop you off somewhere, Elsa?"

"No, no. I shall walk. It is a pleasant night." She thrust her arms into her fur coat.

"Walk?" Tom said incredulously. "To Brookline?"

"She does it all the time," his father said helplessly. "Imagine."

"Well, Eleonora Sears walks to New York," Elinor said.

"But not in the middle of the night," Tom said.

"In Europe we walk a great deal," Elsa said in her most superior manner. "We do not have your motor cars, one to a person. Good night." She bowed stiffly to them and let herself out before the doctor could get to the door.

He looked at Elinor sharply. "Did something happen?"

Elinor felt shaky. "No, except that she told me I should get a job."

"Were you rude to her?"

"Not terribly." She looked at him. "A little. I'm sorry, Dad. She can be so superior . . ."

He flushed. "When you are in my home, you will be courteous to my guests." He got their coats out of the closet and threw them on a chair. "Hurry up. We'll be late." He went out ahead of them.

Elinor was close to tears. She had ruined their Christmas Eve. And she felt even worse about the fact that her father was not on her side. He had always defended her against almost everyone.

They were silent on the way to the station, although once or twice Tom tried to get a conversation started. Their father walked with them to the gate, but he didn't go through to the train.

She faced him. "Thank you for the lovely presents." She paused. "Please don't be mad at me."

He looked at her sternly for a moment and then his expression changed and he put his arm around her. "I'm not. It's just that . . . I'm in such a hell of a position.

You've got to start growing up, Ellie, and understanding other people. Thank you for the scarf. Have a happy Christmas." He kissed her forehead. Quickly he shook hands with Tom. "Let me know when you can get into town." He gave them a tight, painful smile, and hurried away.

On the train Elinor turned her face to the grimy window to hide her tears. When she had them under control, she said, "I'm going to quit school and get a job."

"Don't be silly," he said. "Just because you got mad at Elsa . . ."

"It's not that. I hate her, but she's right."

"There'd be a terrible row. Mother would never let you."

"She'll have to. There's nothing she can do about it."

The conductor came through the car, letting in a blast of icy air. "Salem, Saaa-lem. Beverly next stop."

They were almost in the Beverly station before Tom answered her. "I won't be much good to you, but I'll do whatever I can. Do you want me to help prepare Mother while I'm here?"

"No," she said. "Thanks, Tom, but I'll do it."

CHAPTER EIGHTEEN

On the first day after Christmas vacation, Elinor walked to the railroad station instead of going to school. She had not talked to her mother about leaving school; she had decided she would rather face her with an accomplished fact. She had talked to Miss Jones about it during their plane spotting hours, and to her surprise Miss Jones had been inclined to approve.

"You're learning to read much better," she said. "Those sessions with Mrs. Winslow have helped you a lot. But I don't honestly think school is doing much for you at this point. Later, when you've gotten on top of the reading problem, I'd like to see you find a college that would be good for you. . . ."

"Or that will take me."

"We can find one that will take you. They're not all so tied to the grades-and-exams business. Antioch, for instance, or Rollins down in Florida, or Bennington in Vermont . . . We'll look into all that when the time comes."

Elinor had felt greatly encouraged, as if perhaps after all there might be hope for her having some kind of life of her own. Now she was going to Salem, to the United States Employment Service, which Miss Jones had told her about. It was a government employment service.

The train was full of commuters, men in business suits engrossed in their newspapers. Would working help her grow up and "understand other people?" She had been shocked by her father's comment because she had thought she did understand other people pretty well. She had mentioned it to Jed, but his reassurance hadn't been especially convincing.

"You understand as well as any of us do, I guess," he had said. "Adolescents are famous for being concerned with themselves, aren't they? I suppose we all are."

She didn't want to be concerned with just herself. That was how her mother was, and it turned people away from her. Though her mother did have a lot of friends.

She got her compact and checked her hat. It had a way of getting crooked. She powdered her nose and studied her face critically. She hoped she looked old enough. Her face suddenly disappeared from her gaze as the train plunged into the Salem tunnel. It was pitch black except for the rolls of steam that poured past the windows.

In a minute they came out of the tunnel. The man in front of Elinor hadn't even lowered his paper. He'd just sat there holding it till he could see again.

"Saaa-lem!" The conductor came through the train and picked up the ticket stub stuck into the back of the seat facing Elinor. "Salem, Salem."

She was almost the only one to get off, although a lot of people got on, people with the *Boston Herald* folded under their arms, people looking sleepy and remote, a few girls who looked like stenographers. She wished she knew stenography. But she couldn't very well learn shorthand until she had mastered longhand. Sometimes it seemed as if the whole world was constructed on a knowledge of reading and writing. She climbed down the steep rail steps and walked back up the platform, through the cavernous steamy train shed, to the street.

She found the USES office, just off Essex Street. She had looked up the address in the telephone book.

She stood in front of the door trying to build up her courage. She had never applied for a job before. She visualized being cross-examined very thoroughly, probably having to take tests that she'd have trouble with. She almost lost her nerve and went away. She could just wander around Salem, do a little shopping, until time for school to be out, and then go home and never tell what she'd been about to do.

But then she thought of spending the rest of the year in those classes, and she thought of Elsa's contempt. She pushed open the door and went in.

A pleasant-looking woman said, "May I help you?"

"I want a job," Elinor blurted out. She expected the

woman to say, "Well, what kind of a job? I'm not a mind reader."

Instead she just said, "Good. We need people. What's your experience?"

"None," Elinor said. "I graduated from high school last spring, and I've been taking a P.G. course but I want a job. Preferably in defense work or something like that."

The woman smiled. "I'll bet you've got a brother in the service. Or a boyfriend."

"Both."

She nodded and found an application form. Elinor thought, I may as well tell her right now, so she said, "I'm kind of slow at reading and writing. I'm not stupid or anything, but I got hit on the head when I was young, and it . . . it made a difference about my ability to read . . ." She broke off. Now she'd probably be told to go away and not waste their time.

Instead the woman said, "I'll ask you the questions. It's just routine, most of it. You know how the government is. Let's see . . . Name?"

Gradually Elinor relaxed as she answered the questions: her address, her age, her father's name and business, her birthplace, foreign travel if any, education, previous employment, condition of health.

The woman looked up and gave her a quick searching once-over. "You look like a healthy girl. No problems other than the head injury?"

"No. I'm very healthy." And then she added, "I'm a plane spotter, in case they'd like to know that."

"Fine." The woman wrote it down. She filled in a few more things without asking more questions. Then she looked up and said, "We have some jobs for inspectors."

"Inspectors?" For some reason all she could think of

was the health inspectors who go around peering behind shelves and under counters in restaurants. Or fire inspectors?

"Yes. For the Navy. They've begun a program to manufacture certain electronic material. I can't tell you what it is because I don't know. It's secret. I'll give you the name of the officer in charge. He will be at the factory all afternoon. Here's the address. Can you go over this afternoon, between one and five?"

"Oh, yes." Elinor could hardly believe it, it seemed so easy. But probably the officer would turn her down. Too young or too inexperienced or too slow to see things right. But she thought of what Miss Jones had said about planes. As long as she looked at something and saw it in a way she could identify, that was enough. She prayed it would be that kind of situation.

The woman handed her a card of introduction. "Good luck."

"Thank you ever so much." She wished she could do something for this nice woman. "Thank you."

Out on the street she looked at her watch and checked it with the big clock outside the Daniel Low store. She had three and a half hours before she could see the officer. It was only a short train ride to the factory. The Navy! She wished she could tell Jed, but he was on a train somewhere between Boston and Denver. She missed him already. He and Tom and Miss Jones were the only people who knew what she was doing. She hadn't told her father, although she thought he would approve. But you never could tell about parents. Oh, boy! she thought, wait till I tell that Elsa I'm working for the United States Navy! That is, if I get the job.

Without thinking about where she was going, she

walked up wide, residential Chestnut Street with all its handsome houses built in the Federal and Greek Revival styles for the nineteenth-century sea captains, big stately houses with at least one huge elm in front of each house. She passed Hamilton Hall, an assembly hall built in 1805 and still used for the Salem debutantes' coming out parties. Once she had thought it would be fun to be a debutante, but now it seemed frivolous and silly. All that money spent on one dance, just to say to the world "here's my daughter, who wants to marry her?" I am putting away childish things, she thought complacently. If I get this job, it's going to be the big jumping-off place from childhood to being grown-up.

She cut back to Essex Street and turned toward the shopping area. She was hungry, and ate a second breakfast at the lunch counter in Almy's department store, then window-shopped for a while. When she got tired of that, she went into the Essex Institute and looked at old whaling logs. She got so engrossed in those, she almost forgot to leave time for a sandwich before she took the train.

She sat on the edge of the hard train seat as it pulled into the station. She was the only passenger that got off. It was ten minutes to one. She walked the short distance to the ugly, sprawling factory that had once been a hosiery mill, then a light bulb factory. It was built close to the river, near an old stone-arch bridge. She was still five minutes early so she backtracked and looked at the pictures outside the movie theater. Bette Davis in *The Man Who Came to Dinner*. She wondered if she could get her mother to go to that with her. Only probably her mother wouldn't even be talking to her when she'd heard what Elinor was up to.

The factory whistle blew, making her jump. One o'clock. She hurried back to the gate, where a watchman sat in a little shed out of the weather. He came out and looked at her, wearing his gun. Times had certainly changed. She was sure there had been no watchman with a gun when they made stockings or light bulbs here. She showed him the card the employment woman had given her. He gave her a visitor's badge. "Inside to your left."

She went through the low doorway and turned left. A sign on a door said "United States Navy." She knocked. Her knees felt shaky.

"Come in," someone said.

She pushed open the door and saw a young man in Naval uniform sitting at a desk in an otherwise empty room. He had a long, dark, good-looking face and he was younger than she had expected. About Tom's age. "Lieutenant . . ." she began, and then couldn't think of what else to say.

"Ensign," he said. "Come in. Are you from the employment office?"

"Yes." She handed him the card.

He glanced at it briefly. "Sorry I can't say 'sit down', but I just moved in here and there's no furniture yet." He was very serious.

"I don't mind."

"Mrs. Emery called me about you. You sound all right to me. It's a Civil Service job, you know, CAF-I, which is pretty near the bottom of the ladder. The pay is . . . well, what is it, let's see . . . $1260 a year." He gave her the first small smile. "I'm still pretty disorganized. I just got here yesterday. The work week is five and a half days, Be here at 8:30 A.M."

She was bewildered. "Aren't you going to . . . ?"

"To what?"

"Well, interview me or anything?"

"No, I leave that to Mrs. Emery. You look okay."

It occurred to her that he was not as casual as he seemed. His dark eyes were searching. Maybe it was like a good detective who finds out all about you while he's asking you for a light for a cigarette.

"This is a top secret program, as Mrs. Emery told you. When we sign you up, you'll take an oath not to discuss anything that goes on here. It's an important program and you can feel you're making a real contribution to the service." He got up. "I'll take you upstairs and introduce you to Aggie. She's training our new inspectors. She's the best craftsman in the plant." He suddenly seemed quite chatty, as he led her along the low-ceilinged corridor. "Our program is still in the pilot stage, the engineers are still fooling around with it, so it will be a little while before we get into full production. That means you won't be rushed at first, and you'll get a chance to get your sea legs."

"That's good," Elinor said. "I've never done anything like this before."

"Neither have most of the rest of us. But the Navy is a lot of things besides ships these days."

She thought of Ben and wished she could tell him what she was doing.

He stopped at a door and stood back to let her go ahead of him into a long, narrow room with benches and tables filling most of it. At one table there were about a dozen girls and women working with soldering irons. And at another table sat two middle-aged women who looked as if they belonged at one of her mother's knitting teas; a girl of about twenty; and a chic woman in her thirties who seemed to be trying hard to look self-possessed in an alien situation.

A tall, broad-shouldered young woman with a limp came toward them.

"Got another one for you, Aggie," the ensign said. "Miss . . . uh . . ." He glanced at the card in his hand. "Golden."

"Okay, Ensign Hull." And to Elinor she said, "Sit next to those women."

When Elinor looked up to thank the ensign, he was gone.

"That thing in front of you is a soldering iron," Aggie said. "You're going to learn to solder."

"And it isn't easy," said the gray-haired woman next to Elinor.

"Oh, come on, Bernice, you're a college graduate, aren't you?" Aggie had a tough, badgering manner.

"I never matriculated in soldering," said Bernice.

Quickly Aggie explained to Elinor how to hold the length of solder and the iron. "All right. You heat the iron in here . . ." She pointed to a metal cradle. "It has to be real hot. Then you hold it to the end of the solder stick, like this . . . until the solder melts. Then . . ." She pulled toward Elinor a pair of tiny things that looked like radio parts, miniature size. "We're just practicing on these. You want to solder these two wires right at this point. You have to drop the solder on while it's still good and hot, or you'll get a cold solder that won't hold. Like this you do it." She held the iron to the solder and dropped a small blob of molten solder exactly onto the place she had indicated. "See?"

Elinor nodded.

"All right, try it." Her tone was challenging. In some

way she reminded Elinor of Elsa, although they were totally different in most ways.

Elinor put the iron into the heating cradle. She wondered how she would know when it was hot enough, but she was too nervous to ask. She tried to remember how long Aggie had left it there. She grasped the long string of solder in her left hand, peered at the place she was supposed to solder, and reached for the iron.

"Wait a minute," Aggie said. "Don't solder over my solder. Here, do it here."

Elinor's hand was unsteady as she held the tip of the solder to the iron. When the drop of molten solder fell into place, it looked different from Aggie's, gray rather than silver.

"Cold solder," Aggie said, with a kind of triumphant malice. "Keep working at it." She walked away with her fast limp toward the other table where the second group were working with solder irons.

"She's mean," Bernice whispered. "Mean, mean, mean. I'm Bernice Dodson, and this is my friend Eloise Van Buren."

The woman named Eloise Van Buren leaned forward to say hello. She was lean and gray-haired.

"We've never done anything like this," Bernice said. "We're trying to do our patriotic duty. But she . . ." She glowered at Aggie's broad back. ". . . she resents us. What did you say your name was?"

"Elinor Golden. Why does she resent us?"

Eloise answered. "She's factory, we're Navy. She's used to being the big cheese around here. Now we're over her."

"You aren't Dr. Golden's daughter, are you?" Bernice asked.

"Yes."

"Well, what do you know! Eloise, she's Dr. Golden's daughter. Oh, we love Dr. Golden. He cured my bursitis. Gave me novocain injections and cleared it right up. A lovely man."

"Thank you." Elinor looked at the other girl and smiled shyly. "What's your name?"

"Jill Pfaff," the girl said. "I guess we're all new today."

"We're the first," Bernice said. "They had to get the program going in a hurry. It's a big rush-rush deal."

"I'm Dolly Bigelow," said the woman in her thirties, who sat apart from the others. "And I've perpetrated seventeen cold solders in the last fifteen minutes." She raised her eyebrows quizzically, somehow implying that it was the soldering process that was hopeless, not herself. Elinor noticed that the two older women regarded her disapprovingly and she wondered why.

She forgot about them for a few minutes, as she concentrated on getting the soldering right. It was not as easy as it looked. But after about ten minutes she began to get it. She wished Aggie would come and approve. She kept on working, silently, while the conversation of the women swirled around her. She wanted very much to do this well.

She heard Eloise say, petulantly, "What are we doing this for anyway? We aren't going to be *working*—we'll be inspecting."

Aggie heard her. She came over to the table and leaned on it, staring at Eloise with clear hostility. "If you're going to reject a cold solder," she said, "it might be a good idea if you find out first what a cold solder is."

"I can tell by looking," Eloise said huffily.

"Oh, you can, can you? Well, I don't know about you educated people. Me, I had to learn how to do it before I could criticize what anybody else was doing."

"Learning by doing," Dolly Bigelow said. She lit a cigarette.

Aggie's eyes blazed. "Put out that cigarette!"

"Oh, sorry. I forgot." Taking her time, Dolly ground it out under her heel.

"You're not at a cocktail party," Aggie said.

Dolly smiled. "I can tell."

"And one more thing," Aggie said to Eloise. "If you think inspecting isn't working, you're in the wrong place."

"I meant on the assembly line," Eloise said. She looked at Bernice and shrugged her shoulders as if to say "hopeless."

Aggie looked at Elinor's work. "Very good," she said abruptly, and left.

"My soul!" Bernice said. "I never heard her say that to anyone, and I've been here all day long. You must be a privileged character, Miss Golden."

"Maybe it's because she's good and the rest of us aren't," Dolly said.

Elinor didn't know what to say. She felt pleased with herself, but she didn't want to seem conceited. "I'm better at doing things with my hands than with my head," she said.

They kept on working at the soldering until closing time. It was tedious, but it was also a challenge to get it right every time. Elinor was glad she was not going to be a solderer for the rest of her life. It had never struck her before how deadly it must be for someone on an assembly line who did the same small task day after day.

162

As soon as you got so you could do it well, the challenge would be gone and it would be pure monotony.

Just before they left, Ensign Hull came in and told them to report to his office at eight-thirty in the morning. "You'll be sworn in and get your badges and your assignments." He nodded impersonally and left again.

Dolly walked out with Elinor. "Well, it's a new experience," she said, lighting a cigarette as soon as she got outside. "Smoke?"

"No, thanks."

"Do you have a ride?"

"No. I came on the train. There's one in about twenty minutes."

When she learned where Elinor lived, she said, "I'll run you home. Why don't we make ourselves into a car pool? I can pick you up as easily as not. It'll be company."

Elinor wasn't sure yet what she thought of Dolly, but it would be a lot more convenient than the train. "I'd like that. I'll buy the gas."

"No, we'll split it." She led Elinor to her car, a late model Packard.

It's not the money she's working for, Elinor thought. She said, "This is a beautiful car."

"It's my fiancé's, actually. He's a commander in the Navy. He's at sea now." She made a face as Eloise and Bernice climbed into an old Ford parked up the street. "Those old harpies. They're working because they're broke, but they like to say it's 'patriotic duty.' They live together in genteel poverty in a house on the river road. Pathetic, actually. I see them when I go marketing. They hate me because I'm divorced. What they actually hate is that I attract men; they're consumed with jealousy."

Elinor felt uncomfortable. This sounded like the gossip that went on at her mother's bridge parties, except that Dolly was younger and had more sense of humor than most of her mother's friends. She didn't know how to answer, but it wasn't necessary for her to say much. Dolly just kept on talking.

By the time they reached Elinor's house she knew quite a lot about Eloise and Bernice—a lot more than she wanted to know—and also about Ensign Hull, who was engaged, twenty-nine, and "a sweetheart." And she learned that the project they were to work on had one of the Navy's top priorities, and it had something to do with radios and fire power. It made Elinor nervous to hear about it, since she was not supposed to know what it was, but at the same time she was curious.

"See you at about eight," Dolly said, smiling at her. "Awfully glad you turned up. I was finding that bunch pretty hard to take."

Elinor thanked her and went toward the house with sudden misgivings, realizing that her mother was probably worried about her by now. It was much later than her usual arrival time.

She was right. Her mother met her in the hall, looking genuinely worried.

"Where have you been? I couldn't imagine. Then I called the school and they said you hadn't been there." When Elinor didn't answer at once, she said suspiciously, "You went somewhere with your father. You could at least have told me. I'm here alone, worried sick . . ."

There was nothing for it but to plunge in.

"I'm giving up school," she said. I've got a job as a Navy inspector."

Her mother sat down abruptly in the hall chair. "What?"

Elinor had rehearsed her speech, and now she delivered it, trying to sound reasonable and unemotional. " . . . I'm sorry you worried," she finished. "I didn't know they were going to put me right to work."

"In a factory?" Her mother spoke the word as if it were obscene. "You think you're going to work in a factory? My daughter?"

"I don't 'think,' I am doing it." She turned away, aware all at once of how tired she was. "Let's talk about it after dinner."

Elinor was almost at the top of the stairs when her mother said, "I'll never allow it."

CHAPTER NINETEEN

Dinner was an ordeal. Elinor found it almost impossible to eat, she was so upset. Her mother stormed, wept, threatened, blamed her father, blamed Miss Jones, even blamed Tom.

"You wouldn't have thought of this insanity all by yourself," she said.

"Why not?" Elinor asked wearily.

"You're not a rebellious child."

"Mother, please calm down and try to understand. I'm not rebelling, against you or anybody. We're at war. Everybody else is doing something worthwhile. How can

I have any self-respect if I go on dithering away in high school like a retarded child?"

"I never said you were retarded." Her mother began to cry.

"Thanks a lot." Elinor shoved back her chair.

"You've hardly eaten a bite."

"You've hardly given me a chance. Meals are supposed to be peaceful, aren't they? Otherwise you get indigestion."

"You don't need to be impertinent."

"Mother, I can't win in an argument with you. I just want to tell you again: I have a job. I'm going to keep it."

"And if I forbid it?"

"It won't make any difference."

"You're still under my roof. I can stop you."

"How? Will you send the police to bring me home?" She knew she had a point there. There was no way she could stop Elinor that wouldn't create a public fuss with gossip to follow.

Her mother looked at her a moment. "I was thinking of giving your father the divorce he wants. But if he persists in influencing you to defy me, I shall change my mind."

Elinor whirled toward her mother, her distress and exasperation turning to anger. "That is a dirty trick, and you know it. You did not intend to give him a divorce. You're just trying to blackmail me into giving in. And I have told you ten times, Dad knows nothing at all about this. If you don't believe it, call him and ask him."

Her mother gave an unpleasant little laugh. "You think he would tell me the truth?"

"Have you ever known him to lie?" She wished she could hit her mother.

Switching tactics again her mother said, "You won't be able to handle the job. You've had brain damage."

"Oh, now it comes out. For years you've sworn up and down there was nothing wrong with me because you couldn't bear to have anything wrong with someone that belonged to you. But now it comes out." She took a step toward her mother and noticed with satisfaction that her mother flinched. "If you are so upset about this job, I'll move out. I'll get a room somewhere."

"You have no money."

"Oh, yes, I have. And I'll be earning money. I can get along by myself very well." She waited but her mother didn't answer. "Is that what you want me to do?"

Her mother stared at her with wide eyes, as if she had never really seen her before. "No," she said. She burst into tears and left the room.

Elinor went upstairs and lay down. She felt drained. Was it really she who had said all those things to her mother? She turned on her radio and half-listened to Richard Crooks singing on "The Voice of Firestone." If she did move, she'd take Tom's radio with her. After all, he'd said to take care of it. The idea of moving was a little frightening, although it was also exciting. Leaving home . . . She liked her home. But if her mother was going to act like this, it would be impossible for both of them. She thought about going over to the Winslows' and asking them what she should do, but then she decided it was her own problem, no one else's. She didn't even want to tell her father until the whole business was settled. She was not a child any longer; she had to make her own decisions.

She sighed. If this was growing up, it was a darned

exhausting experience. She took a shower, set her clock for seven, and went to sleep.

Her mother was not up when she left in the morning. She half-hoped there would be a note from her in the kitchen. It was awful being on bad terms with her. But there was nothing. Hastily Elinor made toast and tea and then hurried out to meet Dolly. She had to wait almost ten minutes. She got extremely nervous while she was waiting. What if Dolly were unreliable and forgot all about her or decided against going back to work? Then she would have missed the train and she'd be late to work her first day and Ensign Hull would certainly fire her. The Navy didn't want undependable people. She looked at her watch every couple of minutes. If Dolly didn't show up, maybe she could catch the 8:40 train, and phone the ensign from the station that she had been unavoidably detained. She knew it was no good asking her mother for the car, even under the best of circumstances. Her mother hated to drive, but she also hated to be without her car.

Just as Elinor was getting ready to dash for the station, Dolly drove up, smiling and casual as if she were right on time. "Good morning," she said. "Hop in. Off to work we go." She made no reference to being late. Perhaps she didn't know she was. She chattered about an amusing party she had been to the night before, the people she had met, the attractive men. "But my heart is on the high seas. That's what I tell them all."

Elinor wondered what it would be like to be pursued by dozens of glamorous men, as Dolly seemed to be. It might get complicated.

In spite of her worry they arrived at the plant two

minutes early. After they had all gathered in the office to take the oath, sign their names, and get their temporary badges, Ensign Hull took each of them to their departments. There were four departments, effectively separated so that people who worked in one never got into the others. It was a way of preserving security.

Elinor and Jill were assigned to I-2. Poor Dolly disappeared upstairs with Eloise, while Bernice was taken to I-4, at the top of the building. Dolly had tried to talk the ensign into swapping her position and Jill's, but he wouldn't do it. Elinor was just as glad. She liked Dolly, but Dolly was distracting; she talked so much. Elinor wanted to concentrate as hard as she could.

Ensign Hull introduced her to the head of the line on which she would work, a French Canadian woman, about forty, who looked at Elinor with suspicion. All the girls on the line stared at her, some with hostility, some with curiosity, none with any signs of welcome. We are the outsiders, she thought, the strangers, the people who think they know it all. She could sympathize with their attitude. They were working girls, who knew what it meant to work at a hard job every day, wartime or peacetime. No wonder they resented people who hadn't had any such experience coming in to tell them what they did wrong. She wished she could tell them she'd like to be friends.

Aggie appeared. "This is what you'll be inspecting." She showed her a black plastic rounded shell. Inside it were miniature radio parts: a tiny tube, resistors, a condenser, brightly-colored enclosed wires that she was told were called "spaghetti."

It's a miniature radio, Elinor thought, but she remembered in time not to say it aloud. She had studied the insides of radios out of curiosity about what made such an apparent miracle take place.

"This one I'm showing you hasn't been soldered. When it comes to you, all these connections will be soldered." Aggie's broad finger pointed out the connections. "It's your job to see that the parts are where they belong, and that the solders are strong. A cold solder will break apart."

"Can I study it for a minute?"

"Sure." Aggie's manner was different from yesterday. She was impersonal and businesslike, but she was no longer antagonistic.

Elinor held the thing in her hand and concentrated on it, getting the image in her mind. Carefully she touched the components with the tip of her finger. She was aware that Aggie was watching her curiously, but she studied it until she was sure she had it clear in her mind. She nodded and handed it back to Aggie. "I think I've got it."

Aggie turned away and spoke to the girls on the line. "All right, you guys, get on the ball."

The girls went to work, but they kept up a steady stream of chatter. There were a lot of Greek and Polish families in the town, and while she waited, Elinor watched them, speculating on who was what.

The leader of the line, Jackie, was not vivacious, but she had a lot of controlled energy and, at least with the girls, a kind of hard-boiled humor. She spoke with a strong French Canadian accent, and once in a while she burst into a tirade of French. Elinor didn't always understand her, because of the Canadian accent, but she got the gist of it usually.

The other girls yelled at her when she spoke French.

"Cut out the froggie stuff, Jackie."

"Speak-a da English, Jackie."

And the bouncy little blonde named Josephine would yell back at Jackie in what Elinor assumed was Polish, although she wasn't sure.

The girls were full of jokes and obscenities. Elinor imagined her mother's reaction to them and smiled. They still ignored her in their conversation, but she knew they were watching her reactions. They shouted down the table at each other, badgered each other, insulted each other, kidded each other. Elinor could almost physically feel the waves of their vitality.

The first unit reached the end of the line. The girl who was to apply the final solder held it in her hand, ignoring it while she finished the story she was telling. Her name was Rita. She was a tall, stout girl, with a resonant voice. With great verve and drama she was giving them an account of her husband's beating her up and throwing her down the stairs.

"Hey, he must be a tough guy," Josephine said. "I mean you ain't no feather, Rita."

"He thinks he's tough," Rita said. "You shoulda seen him after I picked myself up and sailed into him. He ain't gettin' out of bed today."

They all laughed, and some of them offered Rita advice, both practical and bawdy.

"Knock it off, you guys," Jackie yelled at them. "Rita, will you get that thing soldered?"

"What's the hurry?" Rita said. "We ain't in production." She heated her iron. "What are these things anyway? I don't like to work on nothin' I don't understand."

"Then you wouldn't work on nothin'," said a small dark girl named Addie Pappas.

"Shut up, Pappas," Rita said good-naturedly. "You think you're some kind of brain or something?" She applied the solder expertly and shoved the unit along the table to Elinor.

They all stopped talking, and Elinor knew they were watching her as she inspected it. She looked it over carefully, taking her time, determined not to be panicked by that watchful silence. Everything was in its proper place and the solders looked good. Without comment she put it in the tray designated for accepted units.

Jackie said something under her breath in French, which Elinor didn't catch. The conversation among the others resumed as they started the next unit. They still ignored her. She wondered how long this would go on. She had never been one to make friendly advances herself until she was sure they would not be snubbed, so she waited for them to show the first sign of acceptance.

Toward noon Ensign Hull came back with a young man in a Chief Petty Officer's uniform, a short well-built man with curly dark hair. They went first to Jill and then came over to Elinor.

"This is Chief Petty Officer Stanley. He'll be in charge of you inspectors." He clapped the CPO on the shoulder. "It's all yours." And he left.

Chief Stanley sat down next to Elinor and picked up the units she had inspected. He looked them over carefully. Then he gave her a friendly smile. "Look all right to me."

She was relieved. It was nice to have him approve, but it was even nicer to have someone smile at her. "Good," she said.

"Everything going all right?" He ignored the scrutiny and the remarks, some of them audible, that he was attracting from the girls on the line.

"I think so."

He stood up. "If you have any problems, holler."

As he walked away, someone at Elinor's table gave a long wolf whistle. Elinor wanted to laugh, but she was afraid it would be disloyal to the Navy. She bent her head over another unit and accepted it. She felt as if she were walking through a minefield. Anything she did might trigger an explosion. But all she could do was concentrate on her job and do the best she could.

The units began coming through faster, under Jackie's prodding, and soon she didn't have time to worry about possible dangers.

 CHAPTER TWENTY

On the way home she worried about going through more scenes with her mother. She only half-listened to Dolly's scathing remarks about Eloise and her complaints about the boredom of "sitting there twiddling my thumbs waiting for those characters to come up with another unit."

"I ran out of aspirin," Dolly said, "and me with a man-sized hangover. And do you think any one of those people would give me an aspirin? They acted as if they never heard of it. Finally, Chief Stanley saved my life. He's cute, isn't he?"

The house was dark when Elinor got home. She let herself in and found a note from her mother saying only

175

that she had gone to Boston with Edith for dinner and the Symphony. Relieved, Elinor fixed herself some dinner and then called her father to bring him up to date.

He was surprised and enthusiastic. "I'll have to tell Elsa," he said. "She'll be impressed."

Yes, Elinor thought, do tell her.

"If your mother gives you a hard time, let me know. I can help out with money or whatever you need."

"I have the money you gave me and my salary. I won't need any help."

He worried about where she would live if she moved out. "Let me go with you when you find a place. I want to be sure it's safe. You know, you could probably stay with the Winslows. They've got a lot of room, and they're so fond of you."

"I know, but I'd rather be on my own." Before she hung up, she promised to let him see any place she was thinking of renting. He thinks I'm a baby too, she thought.

She called Miss Jones to tell her the news and to say that she wouldn't be able to plane spot on Saturdays any more. She hated to give that up. "If someone wanted to swap, I could do it on Sundays."

"I think you'll have enough to do without that," Miss Jones said. "It sounds like a fascinating job. Keep me posted, will you?"

Then she went upstairs and wrote notes to Tom and Jed on the old typewriter, hitting the keys slowly and carefully, tracing the words with her eye as Dr. Winslow had suggested, and hoping they were reasonably right.

She was asleep when her mother came home. When she left in the morning she thought with relief that at least so far there had been no explosion.

That day at work the units came through a lot faster, and she was kept very busy.

"If you think you're busy now," Aggie said to her, "wait till we get into full production."

In the afternoon she rejected two units for cold solders. There was a good deal of grumbling, but no one challenged her. However, she saw Jackie go across the room and say something to Aggie. Some time later Aggie came by, picked up the rejected units, looked at them, and put them back in the reject pile. No one said anything, but Elinor felt a faint glow of satisfaction. She had been right. Being right wasn't going to endear her to the girls on the line, but she wasn't here to win popularity contests. It made her feel good to have found something she could do right. Chief Stanley, who seemed to know everything that was going on, drifted by and said, "Keep it up, you're doing fine."

That night she again braced herself for a battle with her mother. But it never came. Her mother's approach now was to ignore Elinor's job altogether and to behave as if things were just as they had always been. She made no reference to it, asked no questions. Instead she talked about her own day, and a meeting of the Church Guild, where one of the occasional struggles for power was going on. With a sense of unreality, Elinor listened to an account of infighting between Mrs. Fuller and Mrs. Bennett and their respective cohorts. It was so far removed from the life she was now leading.

But the next day when a bitter fight broke out between Josephine and Addie Pappas over what Josephine's boy friend had said about Addie's boy friend, she decided that perhaps people weren't so different after all, only the circumstances. She wondered why Jackie or

Aggie didn't break up the fight, which was getting louder and louder, but then she noticed that both girls were working furiously as they talked, their anger, in a way, translated into the work of their hands. She hoped she wouldn't have to reject any of their work. She didn't want to tangle with either of them when they were in that mood.

Rita had begun to talk to her. The conversation consisted mostly of Rita's questions and Elinor's answers. What, Rita wanted to know, did it feel like to be a doctor's kid?

"It feels fine if he's nice," Elinor said. "Mine is nice."

"He's the one that ran out on his wife," said Georgie, the big mannish-looking girl across the table. She said it to Rita, still ignoring Elinor.

Elinor felt her anger rise, and she struggled to control it. I'd really be up a creek, she told herself, if I lost my temper. That's being a baby. She behaved as if she hadn't heard the remark.

But Rita wasn't about to let go. "Is that right, Navy? Did your old man run out on your old lady?"

"My parents are separated," Elinor said quietly. "If that's what you want to know."

"That's what I wanted to know." Rita did a good imitation of Elinor's voice and accent, and the others, except Josephine and Addie, laughed.

Elinor picked up the unit Rita pushed toward her and inspected it. There was one of those borderline solders that she could reject if she wanted to. Chief Stanley had told her that she could reject anything that was questionable. He had said, "They might as well learn now to do it right. On the other hand these are experimental models, so it's not quite as serious as it would be if they were going to be used in battle." So she had a choice. Her anger made her want to reject it, but if she did, they would be sure to think she was doing it to get even. Ensign Hull had impressed on all of them that they had to be strict but fair and let the chips fall where they might. She let the unit go.

"That's nothing," Rita said in her normal voice, "my old man has run out on me seven times."

"He comes back to get his three square meals a day, that's all," Jackie said. "*Les hommes.*" She made a disgusted face.

"What are them, Jackie?" Rita said, winking at the others.

"Men. Men, men, men."

Josephine and Addie stopped fighting to join in the general discussion of men that went on for fifteen or twenty minutes. Some of the things they said made Elinor laugh. Gradually they began to include her to the extent of glancing at her now and then, even smiling occasionally when she laughed.

When it was almost time to go home, Addie came back from the water cooler and stopped behind Elinor. "Hey, ain't that an old Tom Mix ring?"

Elinor blushed. Why hadn't she remembered to take the thing off? An inspector for the United States Navy wearing a Tom Mix ring!

But Addie said, "I got one of them at home. I sent away for it when I was a kid. Hey, we're twins, Navy."

It was hard for Elinor to believe, but somehow the old horseshoe ring had made her acceptable. Addie sat down and talked to her for a minute, reminiscing about the other Tom Mix souvenirs.

"Remember the slide-whistle ring? And the mirror

ring? My brother had a decoder badge. We used to fight over it."

Elinor said, "My brother had the six-shooter. We used to fight over it, too."

"Is your brother good-looking?" Rita said.

Shyly Elinor said, "I think he's handsome."

"Where is he?"

"He's in the Army. The ski troops."

"There aren't any ski troops," Josephine said.

"Listen, big mouth, the kid ought to know where her own brother is. If she says he's in the ski troops, then there's ski troops." Addie banged her hand on the table for emphasis.

"Break it up," Jackie said. "Addie, come back here and get to work."

Until closing time the main topic of conversation was Elinor's brother. They asked questions, offered their own speculations, argued. And now Elinor was included.

On the way home she said to Dolly, "I like the girls on my line."

"Do you?" Dolly shoved the cigarette lighter into the dashboard to heat it up. "I can't say I'm charmed by mine. They're foul-mouthed, ignorant, and belligerent."

"Oh, mine are, too," Elinor said, "but I'm getting fond of them."

Dolly laughed. "You're younger. You're more flexible."

That night Elinor wrote a short, enthusiastic letter to Jed. "Between us," she wrote, "you and I will win this war." When she was in bed, she lay awake listening to the wind. In some way that she couldn't quite place, she felt that she was winning a war of her own.

CHAPTER TWENTY-ONE

Five new inspectors were added to the staff. One of them, a man, came to Elinor's department to supervise a third line of newly hired workers. Except for Dolly, Elinor seldom saw her fellow-inspectors for more than few minutes, during morning break or the half-hour lunch period. Even Jill was at the other side of the big room, and the only time she had to talk to her was on those occasions when production slowed down because of a delay in the arrival of material. Elinor liked Jill. She was a quiet girl who minded her own business.

The uniforms that had been ordered for the inspectors

finally came. Elinor was thrilled with them. They consisted of a dark blue wool skirt and jacket, a white shirt with dark blue tie, and a little dark blue hat. Elinor especially liked the Navy patch on her sleeve. She went to see the Winslows on the Sunday after the uniform came, and they took pictures of her to send to Jed.

"I think it's fine what you're doing," Mrs. Winslow said.

"My mother doesn't." Elinor was sorry as soon as she had said that. She didn't mean to put the Winslows in the middle.

But Mrs. Winslow just said, "It's hard sometimes to accept it when our children show us they're grown-up."

"You keep up your reading exercises as much as you can, Ellie," Dr. Winslow said. "And by the way they're doing some very interesting work on head injuries in England. I heard about it at a Harvard seminar last week. Meant to call your father. One of the few good things to come out of a war is the speedup in medical research. They're dealing with an awful lot of head injuries—aphasia, dysphasia, and all the rest of it."

"I hope they get somewhere," Elinor said.

"They've got the incentive and the government backing. Something is being done about a much-improved electroencephalagram, for one thing, using the new electronics."

Elinor was interested. It would be funny, she thought, if the kind of work she was doing turned out to be some small help in treating brain injuries.

At the plant the next time the inspectors had one of their occasional meetings with one of the engineers, who tried to explain the principles of electronics, Elinor listened much more carefully. With no basis in physics she had found it hard to grasp what was being said, but now she listened.

When he said, "That gadget you're working on may someday power your refrigerator or your stove," she said, "Could it have any use in checking brain waves?"

Everyone except the engineer laughed. They thought she was being funny. But he said, "It's possible."

Later he asked her why she had been interested in that. She told him about her accident and its results. His reaction was different from anyone else's: he saw it as an engineering problem. She found it a much easier attitude to take than the ones involving sympathy, pity, or, of course, contempt. They had an interesting talk.

On the way home Dolly said, "That was an odd question you asked Pendleton. What did you have in mind?"

Explaining her problem once in the course of a day seemed enough. Elinor just said, "Our doctor was telling me they're doing research with some kind of electronic thing in England to measure brain waves. Because of the head injuries. There are so many."

"Oh." Dolly seemed satisfied. "I like Pendleton. His wife used to buy stuff from Bert and me."

By now Elinor knew that Bert was Dolly's first husband, but she didn't know what "stuff" referred to, and she was too tired to ask.

For about a week there was a marked slowdown in production, not because of the workers but because no material was coming to them. Explanations were never made, so the girls invented their own.

"This junk we've been making isn't any good," Rita declared. "They've decided to throw it out."

"I heard it's a shortage of material," Addie said. "Somebody goofed up."

"It's the Navy way," Jackie said. That was the ultimate disparagement for anything that went wrong. "You hurry up and wait."

"It's a waste of the taxpayers' money," Josephine said, and they all laughed.

"How much you pay in taxes last year, Jo?" Georgie asked derisively.

"I didn't say nothing about me. People's taxes. That's what pays for all this boondoggling."

Their complaints rose to a howl of frustration and irritation the next day when a load of units that they had worked on were returned to them for dismantling. They had to use their irons to heat the plastic containers so they could take out the components. The unpleasant smell of melting plastic added to their discontent.

When Chief Stanley came in, they all directed their rebellion at him. What was the matter with this cockeyed Navy? Why couldn't they make up their minds? Where was Ensign Hull? There was a rumor he'd been fired for incompetence. Why were they throwing away taxpayers' money? And what the hell goes on here?

Chief Stanley held his hands up, waving them. "Help! I'm under siege. Lay off."

They calmed down enough to listen while he told them that what they were doing was an important part of the process. "Nothing is being wasted. Everything will be used again."

"We're being wasted," Rita said.

"No you're not. You're the most important part of the whole thing. We want the best product we can turn out, and that's what you girls and the Navy together are going to produce. And Ensign Hull is a long way from being fired. He's in Washington for a conference. He'll be back next week."

"Him and FDR are cookin' up something," Josephine said.

"It's us they're cooking," Georgie said.

But Chief Stanley's little speech had defused their wrath. They grumbled and argued with each other after he'd gone, but they were more resigned.

"We're all going to get the Navy Cross when this is over," Rita said. "I got the word."

"Double cross," muttered Jackie.

Elinor looked at Jackie's grim face, wondering as she had wondered often, what it was that made her so chronically displeased with the world. She was the only one who didn't air her private life. Elinor knew nothing at all about her. Maybe she had some terrible cross to bear, some personal tragedy at home—a husband who drank and ran around perhaps, since she seemed so bitter about men. But Rita's husband did those things, and Rita seemed to find it mainly a source of drama. People were complicated. She was having dinner that evening with her father; she must remember to tell him she was beginning to think about other people. You just about had to if you were going to survive here. Maybe that was what he'd meant.

CHAPTER TWENTY-TWO

About a week later there was a sudden upsurge in production. Aggie was up and down the lines urging faster work, and Jackie was snapping at the girls with increasing irritability. Although the girls complained, they were obviously happier with something to do.

Elinor was very busy all day trying to keep up with the trays full of units that piled up beside her. When the girls wanted to turn them out, they could really turn them out. She concentrated so hard, she almost shut out altogether the talk of the girls. In the background the newly installed Muzak system played "When You Wish

Upon a Star." The girls sang along with it. Elinor had thought of herself as knowing a thing or two about contemporary pop music, but these kids knew all the words to all the songs.

Aggie roamed up and down the lines, urging them on. "All out," she kept saying. "All out."

Elinor didn't know what was up, but Ensign Hull had come back from Washington all revved up from his conferences with OSRD, which Elinor had finally discovered meant Office of Scientific Research Development. She had learned that, like many other things, from Dolly.

In the late afternoon she rejected three units in a row. Suddenly Jackie was upon her, arguing, fury in her face. Elinor pointed out that two units had their components in the wrong arrangement and the third had a cold solder. Jackie stared at them, glared at Elinor, and stalked back to her place in the line. She summoned Aggie. While Aggie was studying them, Jackie, in a sudden burst of real rage, said in French, "That cow! What does she know? She's just a stupid little kid." Although the girls on the line, and Aggie, didn't understand what she had said, there was no mistaking the tone. Instinctively they all looked at Elinor.

Elinor, who had been listening to Jackie's French for some time, understood her very well. She felt the blood rush to her face. This was the test.

She faced Jackie and said in French. "You listen to me! I know what is acceptable here. I am the person here who says what will go." She wasn't sure her French would get through to Jackie, but she saw that it had. Jackie glared at her and then abruptly turned away. All right. It wasn't nice, but that was the way you handled the

Jackies in the world. She gave Aggie a challenging stare.

For a moment Aggie returned it. Then she shrugged, said, "You're the boss, kid," and walked away. Elinor pushed the rejected units back down the line. It was very quiet.

After a moment Jackie said, "So fix them!"

They were fixed.

Just before closing time Chief Stanley came in and said to Elinor, "Drop in a minute after work. I want to talk to you."

Oh, boy, she thought, this is it. I've antagonized the whole lot. I'll be fired.

When she got up to go, Rita, who had heard the Chief, said, "Listen, kid, don't let him throw his weight around. You're all right."

Georgie, on her way out, gave Elinor a bit of slightly obscene advice that would have curled Elinor's mother's ears. But Elinor found it very reassuring that they were on her side.

Tentatively she knocked at the door of the Navy office and opened the door carefully when she heard, "Come in." Chief Stanley was sitting at Ensign Hull's desk, puffing a cigar, his feet up. "Come in," he said. "Ensign Hull has gone home. Excuse my informality."

Elinor went in and sat down. The office had acquired a couple of chairs and a filing cabinet.

"I love sitting in the big chief's chair," Chief Stanley said. "You know, I've got seven years in the Navy; he's got . . . what is it? . . . ninety days plus whatever he has here. Well, enough of that. I wanted to say that you handled that ruckus very well this afternoon."

"I didn't know you were there. . . ." She was disconcerted.

"I'm everywhere." He grinned and waved his cigar. "I get reports from all levels. You did a nice job there. Sometimes it is necessary to throw your weight around. This is the first time you've done it, and you picked the right time, and you did it very well."

"Thank you." She felt both pleased and bewildered.

"We want to set up a roving inspector. Somebody that covers all the departments. Somebody trustworthy, bright, and able to handle herself. Ensign Hull and I think you're it."

Elinor was overwhelmed. "I don't know if I can . . ."

He interrupted. "Yes, you can. I know all about your so-called problem. Ah, nuts. I couldn't read till I was eleven, and I had no excuse. You are the best inspector we have, and the second one, the number two, is Dolly Bigelow."

"Really?" Elinor was both surprised and pleased.

"Sure. You're good. Dolly is good, too. After all, she has a feel for this kind of thing. But you're better with the girls. Dolly is more intolerant. But, you know, her background with pots . . .

"Pots?"

"Sure. Didn't you know? She and her first husband were hell on wheel with pots. I mean they were potters. One of the things they broke up over, I understand, is that Dolly wanted to do functional stuff, cooking dishes that were good-looking, all that jazz. I'm not up on that stuff myself."

Gosh, Elinor thought, how much I have to learn. All this time with Dolly, and I never knew what she did.

"You want to take it on?"

"Well, if you think I can . . ."

"If I didn't think so, I wouldn't ask you."

189

She grinned. "The answer is yes."

"Okay. So there we have it. You want to go to the movies some night?"

Elinor froze. "That's not why you . . ."

He interrupted. "Look, I'm a career boy. If I offer you a promotion, it's because I think it will do me good in the end. When I ask you for a date, that's another category altogether."

"All right," she said, "but I'd better tell you now that I have a friend in the Air Corps . . ."

"Ah, the hell with the Air Corps. I'm only asking you to go to the movies."

She giggled, thinking of Tom saying, "I only talked to her, asked her for a couple of dances . . ." "Sure," she said, "I'd like to."

"Very good. We understand each other." He grinned and took his feet down off the desk. "How about Saturday?"

"All right," she said. Then she added practically, "What's the show?"

"Well, it's an old Fred Astaire, but I happen to be sold on Astaire. *Carefree* is the name of it, with Ginger Rogers."

"I'd love that," she said. "I love Astaire, too."

"Right. It's a date." He saw her to the door. "But aside from the hoo-de-hoo and all that, you really are doing a good job."

Chief Stanley came a little early on Saturday night. Elinor could hear him talking to her mother, and it made her nervous. Her mother had continued to behave as if Elinor's job were unmentionable, like living in sin. She hoped her mother wasn't being haughty with Chief Stanley.

But when she came downstairs, they seemed to be getting on beautifully. They were both smiling, and her mother looked relaxed, as if she were enjoying the conversation.

On the way to the movies Elinor said, "I think my mother liked you."

"I've got a way with mothers."

On Sunday she overheard her mother talking on the telephone to her friend Edith. "Oh, did you see Ellie? Was it a good show? . . . Yes, he's a chief petty officer. Quite charming. Elinor is doing very well with the Navy, you know. She's just had some kind of promotion . . . No, I haven't the foggiest. They're not allowed to discuss the work, but I gather it's a very vital program."

Elinor smiled and went back to her room to write to Tom. "Mother has just left the ranks of the knockers and become a booster," she wrote. Poor Mother. Sometimes Elinor thought her mother had worse problems than she herself had ever had. Her mother had never learned to bend with life. "My big fat problem," she wrote to Tom, "that I thought was ruining my life doesn't seem very important now. Isn't that funny? As soon as I began to live my own life, the problem began to mlet." She looked at the last word, inked it out, and wrote in "melt." "I think I'll take up golf again in the spring."

CHAPTER TWENTY-THREE

Elinor sat in Dolly's attractive kitchen, watching her "throw together a few odds and ends for our dinner." Actually she was making things that looked and smelled marvelous. She had roasted a capon, and at the moment she was doing something exotic with sweet potatoes, involving honey and nutmeg.

"I really love your house," Elinor said. "This is the prettiest kitchen I ever saw." There were lots of copper pots everywhere, some even hanging from the ceiling. It was an old house, with low ceilings, wide-planked floors, and pine paneling. The kitchen had a fireplace that ran the width of one wall, with all the old cranes still intact. And everywhere there were the dishes and bowls and things that Dolly and her first husband had made.

Elinor picked up a beautiful little sugar bowl and held it in her hands, enjoying the feeling of it as well as the way it looked. "I wish I could do things like this."

"You probably could. You have good potter's hands. I noticed that right away."

"Why don't you do it any more?"

Dolly shrugged. "My ex made off with the best of the equipment. It's hard to get material now. After the war I'll set up a studio again." She looked at Elinor. "Want a job?"

"Oh, it would be fun to try it."

"You've got taste and energy and, as I said, the hands. There's no reason why you wouldn't be good if you liked it."

Elinor sighed happily. "After the war" might be a long way off, but the future had become something she could contemplate now without panic or despair. Tom had said once there were a lot of good things to do in the world besides reading and writing, and he was right. Elinor Golden, Potter Extraordinary. My daughter the potter. She laughed aloud, and Dolly smiled at her. In her own home Dolly was much more relaxed; she didn't chatter so much. Elinor enjoyed being with her.

Dolly fixed herself a drink and held up the bottle to see how much was left. "I had friends over last night. They drank me out of house and home."

"I don't see how you do it," Elinor said. "I hit the bed right after dinner and go sound asleep, I'm so tired."

"Well, you know what Edna St. Vincent Millay had to say on that subject:

"My candle burns at both ends,
It will not last the night,"

Elinor finished it.

"But oh, my friends, and ah, my foes,
It has a lovely light."

"That's me. But my candle will last the night all right. I'm a tough cookie."

Tough cookie. Elinor thought of the phrase again the next evening when she and her father and Elsa went to the opera. All evening Elsa listened in rapt silence, her hands held very still in her lap, her face lit up. Elinor had never seen her like that. She noticed that her father kept stealing glances at her, too. Once he put his hand over her hands, but Elsa seemed not even to be aware of it. When the opera finally ended, she drew a long breath as if she were just coming out of a dream. When the applause began, she lifted her clasped hands, but she didn't clap.

Afterward they went to Old France for butter cakes and coffee. Elsa was still very quiet and far away. It was only the second time Elinor had seen her since Christmas, but it seemed to her that Elsa had changed a good deal. Or maybe I have, she thought. I notice more. Or we all have. Times like these change people. Her father seemed quiet, too. They talked a little about the opera, but Elsa didn't have much to say.

Finally Elsa looked at Elinor and said, "How goes the job?"

"Very well," Elinor said. "I like it very much."

"She got a promotion," her father said.

"Yes, you told me."

"It's not really a promotion," Elinor said. "I mean I keep the same rating and pay. It's just . . ."

"More responsibility," Elsa said.

"Yes."

"That is very good."

That was all she said, but Elinor felt an immense gratification. She had never thought that Elsa would approve of anything she did, ever. It was nice for her father to be proud of her, but for Elsa to approve . . . She felt herself glow with pleasure.

Elsa came with Elinor's father when he took her to the train. They walked her down the length of the train to one of the forward cars.

"Don't sit in the smoker," her father said, and both Elsa and Elinor laughed.

CHAPTER TWENTY-FOUR

Jed came home for four days. Each evening he picked up Elinor at work and they spent the evening together. As soon as she saw him sitting in the old convertible, she forgot that she was tired.

She introduced him to Dolly, and was pleased that they liked each other right away. And she introduced him to Josephine and Rita, who had somehow found out that "Navy's boyfriend" was home, and who were hanging around to get a look at him. The next day they reported to the line that he looked like a cross between Clark Gable and Cary Grant. "Handsome," Josephine said. And Rita said, "Glamour boy." Each day they cross-examined her about him.

"No more goin' out with Chief Stanley," Georgie said sternly. "We're going to see to it, personal, that you're true to the Air Corps."

Jed laughed when Elinor told him. "I'm glad I've got some friends there to look out for my interests."

They went to Revere Beach on a bitter cold night to dance to the Jimmy Dorsey band. Elinor's mother had never let her go there before, but it didn't occur to Elinor any more to ask permission. It was a bizarre dance hall, done in somebody's idea of Egyptian style, with an enormous canopy hanging from the ceiling.

"What a dust trap that thing must be," Jed said, as they danced under it.

"You sound like a doctor."

"Yeah. Well, I'm going to be some day. We'll get married, and you can get a job and put me through college."

She looked up at him. "Is that a proposal? If so, it's one of the oddest . . ."

He pulled her head against his shoulder. "Who needs proposing? Haven't we always known it?"

She had always thought the day she was proposed to, by whomever, would be one of those shining, brilliant days in her life. But actually it was more like twenty-four-karat gold, soft and gleaming. No fireworks, just something very beautiful and permanent and reassuring. She wondered if, without the dangers the war had brought, she would have had enough sense to know she wanted to marry Jed. Her terror at the thought that something could happen to him taught her to know her feeling for him.

197

On Saturday, his last day, they went all around town, revisiting places that had always been favorites. They went up to the hill where they had first learned to ski and watched the kids soaring and sailing and spilling on the icy slope. They had built a jump, the way Jed and Elinor and their friends used to do.

"Remember what a good skier Ben was?" she said.

He nodded. "Good skater, too."

They walked along the crusty bank of the little river where they used to skate. It had seemed much bigger when they were younger. Elinor pointed out the little stone bridge where they used to crouch under the arch and listen to the loud rattle and roar of cars and sleighs crossing above their heads.

"I miss sleighs," Jed said. "Remember the sleigh rides?"

"Yes. We nearly froze to death, in spite of the straw and the blankets, but it was fun anyway. We always ended up going on to Mr. Conolly's and having a hot chocolate.

"Let's go have a hot chocolate at Mr. Conolly's," Jed said.

Mr. Conolly shooed away the boy who worked for him, and made their hot chocolates himself. Then he sat down with them. They told him how they had been visiting old haunts, reminiscing.

He smiled. "You kids are pretty young for the memory lane routine."

"I'm nineteen," Jed said.

"I'm eighteen and a half," Elinor said.

"I know. Kids grow up fast nowadays."

"We have to," Elinor said. "But it would hit us sooner or later anyway. You can't stay a kid forever."

He looked sad for a moment. "I hate to see you all

going off. Hate to see you go, Jed. And Tom. And poor Ben . . ."

"We'll be all right," Jed said.

"Sure you will." He smiled again. "I'm proud of you, I can tell you that. Watched you kids from the days when you'd spend half an hour picking out three cents' worth of penny candy. Yes, I'm really proud of you." His eyes filled with tears.

"Listen, Mr. Conolly," Elinor said quickly, "Jed's going to get his M.D. after the war and he'll send all his patients to you and you'll be rich."

"That's right," Jed said. "And Elinor's going to be a potter, and she'll buy up all your glue."

"Glue!" Elinor burst out laughing. "You don't make pots with glue."

"Well, I've never made pots. What do you use?"

"Adhesive tape," Mr. Conolly said. "She'll buy up all my adhesive tape." He got up and put a hand on Jed's shoulder. "Take it easy, fly boy. I'll keep the chocolate hot for you."

Jed stood up and shook hands with him. "And keep in a good supply of cherry ice cream, all right?"

"All right." Mr. Conolly went off to wait on a customer, and Elinor and Jed left.

"I like people," Elinor said.

"Yeah. There are a lot of swell people."

"You'd better go home now, Jed. Your family will want to be with you awhile before you leave."

"You come, too."

"No. You be with them. There are only a few hours before you have to go."

"All right. But I hate to leave you." He drove her home. "Keep writing."

"Can you read my kooky spelling?"

"Sure, and it keeps getting better." He kissed her. "You're my girl."

"I know. Be careful."

He nodded and ran down the walk to the car. She stood on the steps watching until he was out of sight.

In case readers are curious about what Elinor and the others were working on for the Navy, it was a miniature sending and receiving radio set that fitted into the nose of a shell, so that the shell could be fired and then guided to its target. It was called the proximity fuse. We made it first for England, and it was the important factor in fighting the Nazi buzz bomb attacks on England. The American forces also used it in the Pacific.

In this book there is a time discrepancy. It was some months later that the production of the proximity fuse began at the plant where Elinor worked. I have jiggled the time factor for story purposes.

ABOUT THE AUTHOR

Barbara Corcoran was born and grew up in Hamilton, Massachusetts, the daughter of a doctor. She wanted to be a playwright, and did have a few plays produced in Boston and in college theaters. During World War II, she was first an electronics inspector for the Navy, and after, a cryptanalytic aide for the Army Signal Corps.

After the war, Miss Corcoran went to Hollywood, where she worked as the manager of a Hollywood office of a publicity service, among other jobs. Then, she found Missoula, Montana, where she received an M.A. at the university and fell in love with the state. Later, she taught in Kentucky and Colorado, but returned to Montana, again, to live and write.

For the past few years, Miss Corcoran has been traveling and writing—in England, Russia, the British West Indies and most recently, Hawaii.

Barbara Corcoran is the author of a number of books including: *Sam; A Row of Tigers; Sasha, My Friend; The Long Journey; This Is a Recording; A Trick of Light; Don't Slam the Door When You Go; All the Summer Voices; The Winds of Time; A Dance to Still Music* and *The Clown.*